FORGIVE *Me*

LOVE ENDURES • BOOK FIVE

SUSAN WARNER

FORGIVE *Me*

Prologue

Eighteen-year-old Lincoln Chase had been waiting for the right time to ask Fiona Dunn to go to the prom with him. They saw each other every day, but they always met away from school. He never gave it any thought. To be honest, Lincoln didn't like people much. People never acted the way they were supposed to. They seemed to change as quickly as the weather. That was one of the things that he liked about Fiona; she was stable.

Fiona Dunn was the girl he never thought would look at him twice. She had long black hair that was so black he could see hues of blue in it. She had bright eyes that reminded him of a cat that was always in trouble. Her nose was short, round, and had the cutest trail of freckles across the bridge of it. Even though she swore those would go away one day, he hoped they wouldn't. She wore tee shirts and jeans just like him. To Lincoln, the most attractive thing about Fiona was her brain. She could remember facts, figures, and solve problems quicker than anyone he knew. She didn't make people feel bad about it either.

Yup, today would be the day. He had just left his job as the dishwasher in the local diner and was on his way to meet Fiona at their spot. In Rolling Springs, Florida, there weren't many places to go, a two-stoplight town. A stoplight at both the exit and entrance of the town. The town had some stores in the middle, and the rest was farmland.

They usually met at the stream. A year ago, they found the spot and built makeshift seats so they could talk about their day before they went home. It was odd for her to want to meet on a Friday. Her dad had Fridays off, and according to Fiona, she was still working on her dad about them being together. However, he wasn't going to complain. The sun was up. There was a gentle breeze. It would be the perfect time to ask Fiona to the prom. They'd be in their favorite place. He couldn't have planned it better himself.

Lincoln had walked out of the diner and off to the side until he was at the dirt path that led to the stream and Fiona. As he walked along, he saw a figure, but it was too big to be Fiona. He stopped and looked around to see if he could see Fiona and anywhere.

The figure turned as if he knew him, and it called out to him.

"Lincoln Chase, I'm waiting for you."

Connor Dunn's voice crossed the distance and sent a shiver down Lincoln's spine. Lincoln was a master at collecting data and seeing trends. He didn't need to do an analysis to know this wasn't going to go well.

"Mr. Dunn." Lincoln hoped that his voice didn't tremble. Connor Dunn was a large man. He worked in construction, and he looked as if nothing could hurt him. Lincoln also knew that Fiona adored her father.

She would tell him stories of how he would take her on camping trips, and they would go to amusement parks together.

Lincoln's parents didn't talk to him unless he needed to go to an award ceremony that had a cash prize. His parents didn't really understand him, but they knew he could make money for them.

"Lincoln, we need to talk."

Lincoln took a seat on one of the stumps and waited. He'd learned that when people asked him to sit, they wanted to tell him something, and it wasn't a discussion. He waited. Lincoln was good at waiting. He took in Mr. Dunn's tense stance. The way his arms were crossed in front of his chest and the way he was taking deep breaths told Lincoln this was definitely not a pleasant conversation.

"Lincoln, I want to talk to you about Fiona."

Lincoln nodded. "You don't want me to ask her to the prom?"

Mr. Dunn stopped, and for a moment, Lincoln saw his body relax, and a look that was alike lot pity flashed across his face for a moment. Then he let out a big sigh and took a seat on the other stump that was across from Lincoln.

"No, son, this isn't about the prom."

Lincoln was confused.

"Then, I don't know what you'd like to talk to me about, Sir."

Mr. Dunn spread his hands out and looked at Lincoln.

"There's no way to say this but to do it straight. You know Fiona is a smart girl, right?"

"Yes, sir."

"She's going to go somewhere and be someone. You have to see how that future isn't going to include you."

Lincoln had started to convince himself that taking Fiona to the prom would be a great thing. Lincoln was sure that no matter what Mr. Dunn said, it was really about the dance, and he had built a case that would put him in the best light. He already knew he loved Fiona and people seeing them at the prom would be the beginning of their coming out. He had already gotten a scholarship, and he would go away to school, but he wanted everyone to know they were together. He had it all planned until Mr. Dunn killed his planning sheet.

"Fiona and I are together now, Sir."

Mr. Dunn shook his head. "No, son, you two aren't together. You see, I know about this place because this is where she and I agreed you two could meet so it wouldn't ruin her reputation at school."

"Ruin her reputation? Fiona doesn't care about that," Lincoln said. Although, even to his ears, it sounded a bit hollow. If she didn't care, why did they meet here? He looked around, and all of a sudden, the place that looked like it was a private sanctuary suddenly became the perfect hiding spot.

"I can see you are starting to think about it. I'm shocked a young man as smart as you didn't figure it out on your own. I mean, even now, you know school is basically over. The seniors are hanging out and finalizing their prom dates. I see you are working hard at the diner. You and Fiona aren't hanging out, though. You've got to see that whatever it is that you think you have with her is only good here. What kind of strain do you think you're putting on Fiona?"

Lincoln's head snapped up. "A strain on Fiona?"

"Yes, son, a strain. She's doing her best to make sure you don't feel bad. She likes you like a lost puppy. You know how good her heart is. For the last year, she's had to make her way out here to meet you."

Lincoln was compiling data in his head, and even though everything Mr. Dunn said made sense, it still didn't add up. He knew what he would do.

"I'll talk to Fiona and—"

"No!"

Again Lincoln stopped short and looked at Mr. Dunn. He had jumped up to a standing position. His feet were braced apart as if he were bracing for something. His jaw clenched, and Lincoln could see the pulsing vein on the side of his face.

"This isn't about what Fiona wants, is it?"

Mr. Dunn pointed his finger at Lincoln as he spoke.

"You know if you had been any kind of normal boy, this wouldn't be an issue, but you're not. You're a freak! You're tall. Your hair is so light brown; it looks red like a girl. You're skinny and don't play sports. The worst of it is you tell Fiona that it's okay for her to be a freak just like you. Well, I won't have it."

Mr. Dunn continued, "You are alone. Yeah, we all know what kind of people your parents are. They borrow on Monday and pay back on never-ever day. If she does all that figuring and thinking in her head, do you know where she'll be? Alone like you!

I won't have it. So listen up, son. I'm calling Cal at the diner. He's my fishing buddy. He'll give you a month's wage, and then you need to get yourself up and leave. Your parents have been bragging you have a significant scholarship to some fancy school, go. After today you won't have a job at the diner. If you don't,

I'll have everyone go to your mooching parents and tell them they need to pay up on their debts, or the town will shun them. You'll see their true colors then. Then you'll understand you are truly alone."

Lincoln listened to Mr. Dunn, and he went through the scenarios in his mind. Each one wound up hurting Fiona or his parents. He understood his mom and dad didn't care for him like other parents, but they were his family. The town wouldn't shun them, but the embarrassment would mean a lot to his mother.

The decision was clear. Now Lincoln was just working on the execution. It was odd he wanted to yell and scream at Mr. Dunn, but the truth of it was everything he said was correct. Lincoln loved Fiona because she made him feel not so alone. He loved Fiona because she made him forget calculations, but most of all, he loved Fiona because she loved him and didn't try to change him. However, if what Mr. Dunn had said was true, she hadn't loved him at all, just endured and pitied him.

It could be true. Even Lincoln's parents couldn't find it in themselves to care about him. Why should he expect any different from Fiona?

"Can I say goodbye to Fiona?"

Mr. Dunn shook his head.

"I'm thinking about her, and this should be a clean break. I'll call your parents and make sure they understand. You, son, need to get your affairs in order and leave Rolling Springs. When you are gone, Fiona will have time to do the right thing."

Lincoln stood and nodded and then held his hand out.

"Thank you, sir."

Mr. Dunn looked at the hand as if it were a snake.

"What game are you playing, son?"

"None. This will probably the last time we meet, and I wanted to shake your hand. Fiona is the best of women. If she ever needs anything, you can call me."

Mr. Dunn laughed and then grabbed Lincoln's hand.

"Call on you, son? I don't think so, but I'm glad you understand."

Lincoln turned from Mr. Dunn and looked around. He looked at the towering trees, the sun shining down, piercing the leaves just enough to give warmth but not enough to overheat a person. Lincoln heard the stream behind him, and then he took a deep breath. When that was done, and he'd absorbed those feelings and thoughts, he walked home.

He stayed to the less crowded path and walked alone. No one saw the tears that ran silently down his face. When he passed people, he heard them whisper 'freak.' When he got home, he closed the door and waited. No one came to greet him like Fiona did at their spot. Just like Mr. Dunn had said, he was alone.

There was no sense in prolonging it. Lincoln went upstairs to pack a duffle bag. He'd travel a little before college with his last pay and try to go to places to black out the spot of heaven he'd found in Rolling Springs. More importantly, he'd load up on experiences to bury the memory of the only woman he'd ever love, Fiona.

One

"Welcome to the Seasoned Worker's Introduction to Basic Computer Terms 101." Fiona Dunn turned and began to write on the board. Six students over the age of fifty-eight sat behind her, who, for one reason or another, wanted to get back into the workforce. Two women and four men who had helped her become the woman she was. However, they were also nervous and scared about the new world they had to go back into.

Fiona wanted to give back to the community that had done so much for her. Mrs. Betty Clampsen, a widow, wanted to keep it private that her husband's payments weren't making it, so she was here as a representative for the women from her church who might want to come. She'd declared that she was paving the way for the rest of the congregation.

Ms. Acosta, an auditor, knew her finances needed some infusion as she called it. At sixty-eight, she had a lean body and firmly believed age was just a number. She currently had her sights on a classmate, divorced Mr. Landers, who was a retired plumber. He had a friar's bald spot and a paunch where Speedy, his Jack Russell, took naps.

"I'm going to write three abbreviations, and we'll go through them," Fiona said, writing the words 'CPU,' 'HDD' and 'DVI.' "I'm sure you'll be familiar with at least one of these abbreviations, or you will have heard of them sometime along the way."

She looked over her shoulder and saw several nodding heads and a couple of smiles.

"Great! Let's go over the first one. I'll write down the dictionary definition while you all tell me what it means," Fiona said. Fiona heard the swish of the classroom door but didn't turn around. Although there was a little bit of murmuring, she didn't want the person who'd come in to feel bad. Fiona had a pet peeve about people being late. She understood the class was seasoned and could be a little difficult to move or keep in a place, so she just kept writing.

"CPU, can someone tell me what that means?"

"I know that one," Ms. Acosta called out. Fiona didn't need to turn around because Ms. Acosta had a high-pitched, clear voice that made you look twice to see if there was really a grown woman speaking. "CPU is Chest Pain Unit. I hear it's the latest thing to have in the outpatient places."

Fiona struggled to keep from banging her head against the board when she heard the answer.

"That's a good try, but the real answer is the Central Processing Unit, also known as the brain of the computer."

"Chest pain unit was a good guess," a man's voice said from behind her. She knew it must have been the latecomer. Fiona sighed and then muttered to herself,

"Lord, help us from those who come and then try to teach from the back of the class."

Fiona had just finished writing the first definition when she went on to the next definition.

"HDD, can anyone tell me that one? It's a little harder, but give it your best shot."

"Oh, I know that one. I sat with Sister Lincoln. It's called hereditary desmoid disease. You know she had a lot of tumors, and finally, one did her in. Lord have pity on her soul," Betty Clampsen said. Her voice was great in small sentences, but she talked so slow that in any other circumstance, you wanted to finish sentences for her. Having a debate with her was torturous.

"Not quite, Ms. Clampsen," Fiona muttered. "This stands for the hard disk drive. This is the long-term memory of a computer."

"But I think you're definition is way more important," the man said. He was definitely past his thirties with a voice like that. His voice was deep and smoky and made Fiona think of romantic nights and close relationships. All of those thoughts did nothing but aggravate her as she had no one, and the future didn't look like it was going to suddenly manifest a man. At this rate, her luck was so bad with men that she would probably send a man on his way.

"Let's focus please on the subject at hand. What do you think DVI stands for?"

Mr. Thomas Landers spoke up. He had a friar's cap and was tall. He was also the object of Prudence's pursuit for a partner. That is, if the town gossip was to be believed. Fiona didn't participate in the gossip, but she found it difficult to ignore as she did her training and listened to people talk in her classes.

Mr. Landers began, "I have that. It's deep venous insufficiency. The veins in my legs are awful. It's so painful, and I know it comes from being on my feet for too long, but what can I do?"

Fiona rested her head against the board. It was too much. Some days she felt like she was pushing the town by herself.

"No, Mr. Landers, the definitions should have something to do with computers.

It wasn't the right answer, but I can see where you were going. I'm also really sorry you have that. It must be rough on you," Fiona said.

Fiona had taken enough. She finished writing out the definition, and then she turned to address the late-comer who obviously thought supporting every answer in the group was great.

Fiona turned and spoke at the same time "Listen, I'm going to need you to keep your opinions to—"

She saw him sitting in the back of the class and stopped in her tracks. If there was a way to take back the snippy comments she'd made, she would have. It wasn't some unknown stranger or a random person who came to disrupt her class. No, she hadn't forgotten that face. How could she when it was commonly pasted on magazines with his piercing brown eyes and perfectly cut hair? She always wondered how he kept every hair in place. When he ran his hands through his hair on television, it never broke its formation. Everything about this man was perfect. He was neat, precise, and all together.

Lincoln Chase, techno-millionaire, and according to most, a certified genius when it came to computers. His algorithms had been bought and used in so many programs and industries that some people rumored he was the man behind the curtain, making shifts in the market. He was never caught unaware, and it seemed all-around unfair that he was a health nut who made it a practice to keep his body as fit as his mind. All of those things were true, but Fiona knew a truth about Lincoln the world didn't know. It was a truth she'd learned the hard way and at the age of eighteen. Lincoln Chase didn't keep his word, and he didn't care about anything but himself.

She'd seen him in town a couple times. It was expected. In a desperate attempt to get funding for her reeducation project in Rolling Springs, Fiona had posted a contest of sorts. She had already received grant money to implement the project, but still needed experienced leadership to guide them. When Lincoln called, offering to lead as well as fund the project himself, he became the boy wonder who came back to do right by his hometown.

Even knowing their history, she had to admit he was still a stunning man to behold.

He gave her a small smile, and if she let herself, she'd be taken in by the innocent, guileless smile that said what you see is what you get. But that couldn't be farther from the truth.

"I didn't mean to interrupt. I just wanted to help you out."

Fiona crossed her arms and stood up taller, making sure her ponytail was behind her. "I'm sure you are used to having your way, but if you want to stay, you need to follow the rules."

Lincoln smiled. "I like rules. Rules are my specialty."

Fiona held out her hand. "Hold on there. The rules in this class are made by me."

"I don't think I broke a rule. Is there a rule not to talk?"

"No, there isn't."

"Is there a rule not to help out?"

"No, there isn't."

"Is there a rule to—"

"Stop! You don't have to worry about the rules because I make the rules. In this classroom, I get to say how the rule should be implemented as well. So understand this. These are the class rules. No blurting out of turn. Everyone gets a chance to speak, and if encouragement or clarification is needed, I provide it. Do you understand?"

She expected him to be somewhat dimmed by having this conversation in front of the class. Instead, he just smiled. "You know how to take charge of your class."

"I certainly do."

He stood up. "I'm glad I was here to help you bring out that necessary part of yourself."

"You did no such thing. I—" Fiona stopped herself before she went down the road of arguing in a class. "You know what, Mr. Chase? Whatever your perception is, it's on you. I appreciate you coming to the class, but I think it would be best for us to meet after the class to discuss any issues or questions you may have."

She walked over to the door at the front of the classroom and opened it. With a smile still on his face, Lincoln walked over to her. He jeans fit him in such a way that could turn the head of every female and a shirt that outlined a lean muscle structure. As he approached, she noticed he was taller than she remembered. All her observations meant nothing. It was a man's character that mattered. Fiona knew Lincoln's character wasn't worth a nickel.

Besides, there were several good reasons that looking at him as a possible romantic interest was unwise. After being in two failed relationships, she didn't trust men. If she decided to give a man a chance, it wouldn't be one who had hurt her before.

She'd have to be a glutton for punishment and disappointment to allow herself to be attracted to him. She was sure his life had changed, and he wouldn't be interested in some small-town girl. With all of that money, he was probably looking or someone in the same status and income range.

Once upon a time, she had dreams of going into finance, but those dreams, like so many others, had been halted when her father had suffered a stroke. Her mother had been gone by then, and she was his only option. Fiona went back to school and got a degree in education and ran for the town office. She might not be able to go where she wanted, but she wanted to use her skill sets to help her town and her father. Fiona was on the planning committee, and she was the town treasurer. She had taken her love of numbers and made do with the situation that she had at hand. She was a self-sufficient woman who counted on herself and didn't need to trust anyone.

"Ms. Dunn?"

"Yes?" she replied with her arms crossed over her chest.

Lincoln widened his smile and looked at her crossed arms. "I want to leave Ms. Dunn, but I'm going to have to ask you to step aside, so I don't invade your personal space."

She looked at Lincoln and then at the other members of the class. They were all waiting with eyes fixed on them two as they spoke. "Of course, I wouldn't want to get in your way."

"There's no problem." He said with a smile that widened enough to show that he had dimples. "I'll see you at the office."

The office? A haze of confusion clouded her mind for a moment, before clearing. He had been the one to "win" the project for the town, and could, therefore, show up at the planning office whenever he felt like appearing. To be honest, she thought he would just delegate the task to someone. "If I'm there when you show up, sure."

Lincoln tipped his head to her and then turned to the class. "It's been an honor to be in your company, madams and sir."

The women stood up straighter and waved at him. Mr. Landers crossed his hands over his paunch and smiled back. As she left the class, she watched them turn to one another, catching the snippets of the banter commending him on his manners. She could tell everyone's attention was done for the day, and she gave them her best smile and let everyone go. She said she'd be here tomorrow, and they'd go over the terms again.

As soon as they were gone, she packed up her belongings and walked to the fruit stand a block away, where she picked up a bag of grapes. She wasn't always this smart. She used to self-medicate with sugar, but now she was older and had a severe aversion to working out. She now self-medicated with fruit. She wanted the fruit to give her something else to focus on. Something besides Lincoln. She needed to either take a vacation or go out more. Because before he turned to the class, he'd given her a smile that looked genuine, and a little spark of something had flared up.

No. She shook her head to herself. It was probably just heartburn. She couldn't allow herself to believe that she was attracted to Lincoln, that would be ridiculous. The feeling had lasted less than a second, a puff of air, the butterfly brush of something. It didn't mean anything. And if it did, so what? She could be attracted to a man who looked good, even if he was a dishonest snake in the grass.

Animal reactions had no morality, so she could attribute it to the fact that she was still a woman and let it go. Lincoln had started here and had decided to leave and go conquer the world, so she knew there was nothing and no one here for him.

Although he wasn't for her, she was glad her inner-woman alarm still worked. It was just off base. But why was he the only person who seemed to set off her alarm?

Two

Lincoln had arranged the meeting in a renovated storefront that used to be a real estate office. Lincoln found it funny because the only land around Rolling Springs was farmland or property passed down from someone else. He had decided to renovate the storefront to conduct the meetings to tell the people of Rolling Springs the plans for their learning center.

Lincoln didn't usually do presentations. Today would be no different. He had sent the slides to the town advisory staff overseeing the grant, and today he would just get their signed copies and then get the work done.

Now that he was in the office and he saw them filing in, he felt a nervousness that hadn't plagued him since he wrote his first algorithm out of college. Lincoln didn't like groups, didn't like people, and wasn't fond of being out of his comfort zone. It was a testament to how much he loved Fiona that he was even here.

His original thought was to have a project manager present the slideshow, but his executive assistant Grace Pattings assured him that he needed to have a more hands-on approach if he wanted to win Fiona.

After attending a reception for a business associate, he realized his life was missing someone. Not a nebulous person who would one day come into his life. The person who would make his life meaningful and engaging would be the woman who held his heart, Fiona. After explaining the history to Grace, they both put their heads together on how to woo her back into his life.

Lincoln had kept tabs on Fiona during the years. He was determined to be there if she or her kids should marry or need anything. Grace would often tell him how rare he was to believe in true love. She thought she had already had her one true love. When Grace husband passed, she went back to work, and Lincoln hired her. The two of them needed each other in ways that went beyond work and were like a surrogate family.

Then, Fiona was petitioning for an adult learning center in Rolling Springs. Lincoln had learned about it two days before the town planned to announce the company they had awarded the partnership to. He'd had Grace call Rolling Springs to outbid their selected candidate. Lincoln donated the amount of money to the other company that they would have made on the grant. He then told the Rolling Springs advisory board to keep the money, promising to pay for the center himself. The committee was impressed by Lincoln because the monetary outlay was negligible. It was one of the few times he used his wealth to help him along.

After this meeting, he could focus on Fiona. Irma Smith and Dione Montalvo walked into the room, and Lincoln's thoughts on telling them how this was going to go fled as they took a seat.

Irma Smith was a short, rotund woman. Her short hair had been dyed once too many times, if the frayed tips were any account. More importantly, she was his retired school principal and had been one of the first to recognize he was special and not a slow learner.

Dione Montalvo was tall and carried herself as if she were walking with a book on her head. Her back never seemed to bend, and when he was growing up, the kids used to wonder how she managed to get in and out of bed because no one could imagine her bending. Now here she was, the retired librarian and one of the two people he was supposed to deliver the plans to.

"Have a seat, Lincoln. You make me nervous standing over there," Irma said as she settled herself into her seat.

Lincoln sat down in the seat in the front of the room. He opened his arms, hoping it would be a welcoming gesture to the women. At least, that is what he had read in the books about body language. The book had said making yourself look larger gave women comfort.

"Hello, Ladies. I want to go over—"

Dione held her hand up, and Lincoln stopped on the dime.

"Listen, I know you were thinking this was going to be a presentation about what you think you can do. However, after we looked at what you sent over, we have decided that you need some help."

"Help?"

Irma nodded. "It's true. You need help, Lincoln. First, we read the proposal, and it just went so fast and beyond us. Before we tell everyone else, we need to discuss how to execute the presentation."

Lincoln sat back in his chair and looked at both women, who looked like they'd made up their minds about the situation. But wasn't it his job to present the information?

"I know the plan may have looked overwhelming, but when I explain—"

Irma shook her head and smiled at him. "No, Lincoln, it wasn't overwhelming. It was just wrong."

"Wrong?" Lincoln knew he sounded like a parrot. He wanted to say he'd been doing this for years. He wanted to explain that this was a small project, and that they didn't really understand how it all had to work. Instead, there was only one word that came out of his mouth. "Wrong?"

Both of the women looked at him and smiled.

Dione sat back in her chair and crossed her legs as she wiped away some phantom piece of dust.

"I am so glad you are taking this so well. You know, there were other people in the town who insisted you would come here with your big-city ideas and try to get us to work on your timetable, but I told them that you wouldn't do that."

Irma nodded in agreement. "Yes, she did. I have to tell you I wasn't sure either, because, you know, when people get older, they think they know a thing or two. But Dione was sure that your good breeding would show and that you would respect our opinions."

Lincoln wasn't sure where this was going, but he knew this feeling. It hadn't happened to him in a while, but he knew this feeling. It was the feeling that snaked through your body and pooled in your gut and told you to prepare for something that you probably didn't want to do. He often had this issue with his parents.

His father had passed away, and his mother traveled the world, but he had never forgotten this feeling and used it to back away from bad deals.

"Ladies, I appreciate—"

Both of the women stood up and smiled. Dione pulled a pamphlet of her own and held it in front of her like a shield. Both women walked toward him and stopped before him.

"We can see that you put a lot of work into the projection," Dione said in a calm voice.

"Yes, Lincoln, your figures were very conservative, and the roll-out plan was easy to follow. We have gone through the document and made the necessary changes. I'm sure you'll agree once you've had time to review it. You were always a smart boy," Irma said as she gave his shoulder a tap.

Dione handed him the pamphlet. "Everything you need is in here."

Irma let out a sigh and stood up. "Well, this was a great meeting," she said. "We want you to know that we are so happy that you came back to help your town. It says a lot about your character." She turned to Dione. "Don't you think so, Dee?"

Dione nodded and then patted Lincoln on his shoulder. "Yes, it does. You let us know if you have any questions, and we will let everyone know what the plan is." With one more nod of agreeance, both of the women walked out of the room.

Lincoln looked around the room and tried to understand what had occurred. He flipped through the pamphlet and read in shock. They had taken his plan and added multiple "work gates", like their approval of the teachers and the curriculum. He flipped on to a couple of other pages and found a page that said he would need to pay a stipend to the first classes so they could get into the habit of coming to school.

He closed the pamphlet and looked around the empty room. He thought about the numbers and figured the budget had just tripled with these "work gates." He stood up and shook his head.

The things a man will do for love, he thought to himself.

Three

Fiona checked her camera around her neck. Then she patted her back pocket to make sure her phone was there just in case. "All set," she muttered to herself.

This was her midweek routine. She would wake up right after sunrise and take a walk through town. She loved this time of the day. It wasn't too hot or too cold. It was the perfect weather for a light jacket. The morning dew would still be wet on the grass, and then birds would greet her as she walked by. What was most important was she was alone and could think things through. Now that Lincoln was here, clear thinking was a scarcity.

She turned to make sure the building was locked. She taught and worked out of a one-story home that had been renovated into three offices and a classroom. The town had given her an office since she addressed the treasury. The other rooms were full of file cabinets and seven-to-ten years of historical data.

After checking the door, she turned to the ramp to begin her walk, and that was when she saw Lincoln walking what looked like a small bobcat but with more fur. He waved and walked over to her.

"Hello, are you going to start your walkthrough?" He asked as the animal that looked like a cat looked at her and seemed to size her up. "We'd like to go with you, if you don't mind."

She thought about saying no but then gave a second thought to doing anything that would upset the creature that appeared to be sizing her up. Her concerns were interrupted by Lincoln's small chuckle.

"Sorry, don't mind Aster. She's harmless," Lincoln said.

As if on cue, the animal looked at Lincoln and then walked over to Fiona and rubbed her body against her leg. Fiona was thrilled and horrified at the same time. She could see the animal was affectionate, but there was way more muscle that rubbed against her leg than she thought there would be.

"This is a—"

Lincoln bent down and ran his hand from head to tail on the beast. "This is Aster. She's a Maine coon cat, and we rescued each other."

Fiona nodded. "Aren't these like the last natural predators in North America for a cat this size?"

Lincoln stood up and shook away the tumbleweed of hair that he had in his hand. "Really? I didn't know that. I don't think that applies to Aster. She wouldn't hurt a soul."

Fiona took that moment to look at Aster, who was indulging in a stretch. When she extended her front legs, Fiona got an opportunity to understand just how big she was. It brought no sense of reassurance when she saw all ten of those claws extend and scrape against the floor as well.

She got ready to tell him what she thought about

his harmless cat when she saw him looking at the cat with adoration and love. Lincoln had a smile on his face. The smile took away the somberness she often saw in his eyes. Even as a teen that somberness had been there. She hadn't remembered that he had a dimple that was so deep it was as if someone had put it there artificially.

When she looked away from his face, her eyes fell on his maroon shirt that hugged his body and suggested he did something else besides sit in an office all day. Her eyes followed his tapered torso until she was looking at muscular legs covered in jeans.

"I'm going to walk through Main Street. If you and Aster don't mind the walk, it's fine by me."

The smile that had been reserved for Aster was gifted to her, and once again, she saw the boy she used to meet by the stream. "I think Aster and I can walk. You know we have sidewalks in the city as well."

He turned and guided Aster to the side so she could continue down the ramp. The motions were obviously something they did all the time. Once she got over the sight of this man walking his cat, she found herself examining Lincoln. When they were younger, she had to admit what intrigued her about him was his brain. He was the smartest person she knew. They talked about everything back then. Now that she was looking at the grown-up version of Lincoln, she had to admit that he had indeed developed some other exceptional qualities. When man and cat walked next to each other, you could see the symmetry of two beautiful creatures side by side.

Fiona mentally kicked herself. This was Lincoln. Lincoln, the man who left without ever looking back.

This was Lincoln, who had been seen in all of the ritzy magazines with so many different women on his arm at charity events that the news had just started calling the women days of the week because their names changed so much. Yes, she'd go on a walk with Lincoln, and when she did, she was sure she'd find the old Lincoln who didn't hang around and who couldn't be trusted.

Lincoln looked up and stared back at her.

"Don't worry, Aster is harmless. If she didn't like you, she would have never rubbed up against you and said hello. Besides, you're not going to get distracted because I have a cat, are you?"

"You have more than just a cat. Other cats don't have reinforced harnesses. However, I don't plan on altering my plans at all. So let's go."

She walked down the ramp and then walked so she was closest to the street. That way she could make an escape if the cat went wild. However, three steps in, Lincoln stopped and waited for her to walk ahead and then walked to the outside. When she saw he wasn't going to let her walk on the outside, she sighed and continued in step with him.

She split her attention between looking at the building and keeping an eye on him.

"It's a great time to do an inventory," he said as they continued to walk. Then a couple of steps later, he cleared his throat. "You don't see a whole lot of people on the streets."

"Are you really going to try to have a conversation as well as busting in on my time?"

"Well, I'm already here. No, sense in wasting time, don't you think?"

"I think it's never a waste of time to let me think."

Lincoln sighed. "I always admired the way you thought. You were always thinking outside of the box."

"I know when it's the right time to think outside of the box, and when it's not. Like when we were in the class. That wasn't the time to think outside of the box. In fact, you weren't being accommodating at all."

"I was just validating their thoughts."

Fiona sucked her teeth. "Validating their thoughts? We were in a class that was going over acronyms that they need for basic computers, and you were concurring with them on acronyms that don't mean a thing."

"I know it made them feel better and helped them to be more involved in the class. Truly I don't mind helping you out at all."

She looked over at him and saw he had a pleased grin on his face. There was no way she was going to be able to work with this man. They hadn't even made the end of the block, and already she was trying to weigh the risk of pushing him over and having Aster the protector cat defend him.

Fiona took a deep breath and let it out as she looked over the buildings. Her mornings were designated to get some exercise, and at the same time, look over the premises to see if any improvements were needed on the lawns of the storefronts or brownstones. She always took a look at gutters and drains to make sure they didn't need any work. If any of the town buildings required work, it would come from the treasury. The hope was she could catch the prospective damage before it became a considerable expense.

She saw one of the gutters on a store needed some help, so she took off her camera and took a picture so she could look at it later. When she replaced her camera on her neck, she realized she had just stopped and hadn't even told Lincoln.

"Sorry, I should have told you I needed to stop."

Lincoln shook his head. "It's no problem. Aster is used to taking cues from me and adjusting."

"You two must spend a lot of time together."

Lincoln smiled. "Aster is my best friend. We are almost never separated, and she travels with me as well."

"Why are you back here, Lincoln?"

"We all need to come home at some point. I'm not the same person I was, but I think there are some things I left undone here."

She glanced over at him as they walked. "You're here to fix the past?"

"No one can fix the past. I'm here because I wanted to do something for my home town. I also wanted to come back and see if it was the same as I remembered it."

"Well, I'm sure everyone in the town will be thrilled you are helping out. They'll want to give you all the help they can."

"Oh, yeah, I've already gotten some "direction" on how to run the project."

Fiona chuckled. "It sounds like Ms. Smith and Ms. Montalvo have given you the corrections they saw were needed in your plan."

"You know about them?"

"Oh, everyone knew. We had a town meeting, and when they went over their corrections, several people asked them if they should wait. They assured the town that you would be reasonable, and there was no need to waste time."

The had walked a couple of blocks when they saw a a table and a couple of chairs outside a coffee shop. "Why don't we take a seat?"

"Okay." As soon as they sat down, a young woman came out, took their order for coffee, and Lincoln requested a small bowl of water for Aster.

They both sat across from each other under an umbrella that gave them enough shade to make it seem like they were in a private area for two instead of on the sidewalk. When Lincoln bent down to give Aster her water, Fiona was entranced with how gentle he was with her. When he sat back in his seat, he looked refreshed and free. There was something about him now that called to her, and she had to swallow and remember who she was sitting with. She had to ignore the width of his shoulders, how strong his hands looked around the coffee mug, and how the errant breeze brought the smell of clean soap and man to her. She shifted in her seat in anticipation. She wasn't sure what she was waiting for, but she had to get control of the situation.

"You must be eager to get back to your life."

"Not really. I can be away for a while."

"I know you wanted to do something for your home town, but I've seen all of the places you've visited in the paper. I mean, everyone has. It's like that when someone from a small town makes it big. Rolling Springs must seem boring to you."

"Nope, I'm a quiet person."

Fiona looked at him, and for a moment, she almost believed him. He didn't look like a man who wanted to leave a small hick town. Lincoln seemed content in a way she would have never thought he would be.

When she saw him now, she would be on the verge on believing what she saw and giving in to the spark of hope that wanted to reach out to him and see if he was real. If she let her heart believe he was genuine and content with Rolling Springs, she'd have to trust him.

Fiona wasn't sure she was ready to trust a man again. Twice she'd thrown her hat in, and both times the men turned out to be something else. Fiona knew some people thought it was because she wasn't interested in sleeping with a man to help "build" a relationship. Fiona suspected the real reason was she didn't want to leave Rolling Springs. There was a time in her life when she had been waiting for prince charming to come and sweep her away, but that time had passed. Now she needed to stay here with her dad, who wasn't in the best of health, and she had made a place for herself here. She wanted a man who wanted to make Rolling Springs their home. The problem was, the only man she had found who looked like he might want the same thing was sitting in front of her.

Four

"So when did you go into public office?" he asked.

"Public office? This is Rolling Springs. It basically just fell to me."

"You mean they all noticed you were ridiculously smart and went with a sure thing?" he said with a smile.

"Well, most of the people who grow up here leave. So there isn't a large bumper crop of kids to pick from."

Lincoln absently leaned down and stroked Aster. He kept his smile on his face when he answered. "I'm sure you were everyone's first choice, Fiona."

"What?"

Lincoln held up his hand. "I know you. You were everyone's first pick." He saw the slight blush of color come over her cheeks, and he had to curl his hand around the mug not to reach out to touch her. This was his Fiona. He'd been around so many "business" associates he'd almost forgotten there were honest people.

"Enough about me. You want to tell me how you become this uber-rich guy?"

He moved his coffee cup around. Then he let out a sigh.

"I don't know. I look at problems, and then I mathematically translate them into algorithms for computers, and then I sell it to others. I give them a little bit of logic so they can learn as they go alone, and they help businesses grow in their own right."

"And it just comes to you?"

"I'm sorry to say there isn't some glamourous story. It does just come to me."

"Then the money came as well?"

"Yes, the money came, but it's a bit overwhelming. One day you are nobody, and then the next day, you have people who want you to look at things so you can tell them what you see. In the beginning, I thought they were teasing me. I even hung up on some people who I thought were pulling a prank on me because I couldn't believe it."

"I read somewhere your brain had already been promised to science, and that they paid you for it."

Lincoln laughed. "Yes, it's true. I mean, when I die, I won't need my brain anymore. In the beginning, the contract for my brain was so restrictive. I couldn't play sports because it might hurt my brain or cause some other kind of injury. I needed to live, so I renegotiated, and now a place will get my brain and sell off slices for charity. I hope to settle down, though, so I'm not so worried about hurting my noggin."

"You say you want to settle, but with all of your money, I imagine you want to settle in a place like Dubai or wherever it is that the filthy rich retire."

"Being rich gets old quick. You do all the things you dream about in the first two or four years, and then the rest of the time, you know you have money and the time to do whatever you want but no impetuous."

"Being here, you don't miss someone waiting on you hand and foot?" she asked.

He shook his head. It was odd. As the conversation went on, he felt her tone change. Even Aster swished her tail and looked up at him wide-eyed.

"So, you're here because you're bored?"

As she asked the questions, it felt like there was a case being built against him, and he was the last to know.

"I'm here because I want to be here."

Fiona shrugged. "I guess that's true until it's not, and then one day, you get tired of the small-town politics, country fairs and church socials."

"As a bachelor I'm always a big fan of food being cooked by someone else and a party. I've done all the other things already. That life that you think is so boring is what I'm looking for."

He wanted to reach across the table and place his hand over hers. Find a way to let her know he didn't just want a life in Rolling Springs. He wanted Fiona. Just when he thought she was going to say something about them, she called for the check.

"Fiona?"

"Well, I hope you find what you are looking for. I need to finish up the walk for the day. I'm already behind." After the waitress had brought the check, Lincoln managed to reach across and grab it. Fiona looked at him with pursed lips and then stood up to leave. Just then a breeze came by and lifted her hair from her shoulders, making her look like a standing warrior woman. She had stepped into a slice of light, and the effect made it look like she had come to earth as some ethereal creature. For Lincoln, it wasn't that much of a stretch. Fiona was the goal in his life, his end game.

"Maybe we could meet again tomorrow?"

She paused and then shook her head. "I don't think that would be a good idea."

Lincoln had to stop short of his next words. He was so sure that she would accept, he was already on to suggesting breakfast.

"Why don't you think it will be a good idea?"

"I think it's hard for people to do things with someone when they're not sure of the person."

"Not sure of the person?" Lincoln echoed.

"Yes, people like you come and go as you please because you can, but it can be stressful to be around someone you don't know."

"Don't know?"

Fiona fidgeted, then looked around before folding her arms over her chest.

"You know what I mean, Lincoln. You have money. You could be gone whenever you get bored. It's hard to count on someone with those options. Money is a great thing to have, but when you don't have it and someone else does in such a large quantity, it makes it hard to trust them. And who wants to be looking over their shoulder every time to see if that person has gone?"

Fiona shrugged, and then she left. He didn't follow her. Instead, he sat back in his seat. It felt like the first time he had been in a fight, and the football captain had punched him in the gut. The breathlessness was there. The shock that it had happened was there, but most important, was the hurt. She hadn't even given him the chance to prove himself. He had just been judged and sentenced by the woman he loved, and the only crime he could see was he had money.

Lincoln could figure out problems, but even this one seemed beyond him.

Five

Fiona needed her schedule like people needed air. Every day she woke up at five a.m. She got dressed, ate a banana or an apple, and then came to the office in order to take her walk. The walk through town kept her fit, her mind alert, and started her day off with a calm that she could call on if needed throughout the rest of the day.

That would have been the truth on any day but this one. Today she wasn't able to get in the right frame of mind. Today when she walked out of the door, instead of the anticipation of going on the walk to work through her stress, her mind was preoccupied with thoughts of Lincoln.

She had reviewed the conversation yesterday, and she could admit that she had been wrong. Fiona recognized that she was feeling boxed in, but she had handled it poorly. Instead of dealing with the issue, finding Lincoln just as attractive as she had as a teen, she decided to push him away. Fiona recognized that she pushed others away before she could get hurt. If she were honest with herself, she'd know it had started the night her one true love had left, the night she'd found out that her father had been a part of it.

When she closed the door to her office, she saw Lincoln across the street with Aster. Her gut twisted in anxiety. She had to find a way to deal with this feeling she had. She had to find a way to deal with Lincoln. While scenarios ran through her mind, the man in question turned and saw her at the door. He nodded and then patted his pockets before turning back to the brick building he had come out of.

She thought she had chased him away. Fiona closed the door, went down the ramp and then looked over to see Lincoln exiting the brownstone again with Aster. Fiona took two steps on the curb when the weight of guilt made her look over. Before she could rationalize it, her feet were carrying her across the street. Fiona believed in treating everyone right. She didn't think because someone had done you wrong that you should return the favor. She felt a person had to hold on to their beliefs and values. It was that thought that had her across the street, facing Lincoln. If she thought standing there would elicit a response, she was mistaken. Instead of greeting her or smiling, he just stood there with Aster, looking back at her.

Taking a deep breath, she stretched her neck and then looked him straight in the eye. "I wanted to talk to you about yesterday. I was wrong to say that to you."

She wanted to fidget under his gaze. How different it was from yesterday when there seemed to be a warmth that pulled her in. Nervously, she shifted from foot to foot. Fiona looked down at the cat, hoping to be distracted, only to find Aster sitting on her haunches giving her a look of disdain.

"Listen, I said I was sorry, so meet me halfway!"

"Wow, I thought I had a problem with people."

Fiona gritted her teeth and tried to calm down. "I'm sorry. I shouldn't have said it. Do you accept my apology or not?"

"I guess so, since you've made the effort to give it to me."

"Fine, I'm glad that's over. You wanna walk with me or what?"

"Ahh, I tell you it's got to be your sweet words and sugary delivery that pulled me in."

"Come on, and let's walk before your cat decides you don't like me."

"Aster is a queen. She's also the most gentle animal I know."

"She's a Maine coon cat. I've been reading up on them. If she's the gentlest animal you know, then you may not be as well read as you think."

"Will you help me with the changes that were suggested to the plan?"

"I don't think they were suggestions, but yes."

"That'll be part of the help explaining what will be done."

Fiona gave him a long look and then faced forward and continued walking.

"I can tell you this. If you can show you are doing it in the best interest of the town, there won't be a problem. Also, if you are willing to be out there and working with everyone, there won't be a problem."

"You don't want to give me a break considering I came in and helped you in your class?"

"Ha ha, no. There are no breaks, and I don't do those kind of deals. We all work hard, and we work for the goal."

"It's good to know there are still people with a good foundation."

"If by good foundation you mean I can't be bought or finagled, then yes I do. We didn't have a large grant compared to other towns, but there were a couple of unscrupulous people who came by and offered me a slice of the grant and then said they would do the project over years instead of the three months we requested. So, my good foundation has been tested."

"Well, I'm not one of them, and my foundation hasn't changed."

Fiona shook her head when she realized they were once again by the coffee shop, and she hadn't been looking at a single thing as she went along.

"Okay, I have work to do, and I think this is the midpoint where you turn around and take Aster home," she said as she pointed to the coffee shop.

"So you're looking after me and Aster?"

"Don't get your hopes up." As if there wouldn't be a number of other single women in the town who wouldn't want to take him on. "You and Aster don't need anyone to look after you. I think the two of you can definitely hold your own."

"Thanks," He said with a wide grin.

Were men born knowing how to smile like that? He had the kind of smile that made you look twice. It was the smile that said come hither. In fact, the longer Fiona looked at Lincoln, she could feel herself kind of leaning toward him and a smile curving her own lips. An errant word brought her back to reality, and she shook her head and stood up straight. The only thing she remembered after that was saying goodbye and making sure not to look over her shoulder.

After she was safely two blocks away, she let out a deep breath. This was not the way she thought it was going to happen. Who could have anticipated that Lincoln would cause that slow, smooth feeling that flooded her body in waves and made her smile for no apparent reason? She hadn't taken the time to actually review the proposal that was given to Lincoln. Now she hoped that Irma and Dione weren't as nitpicky as they usually were and hadn't put in as many changes. If those two women had been as true as they normally were about details, these next couple of weeks were going to be a real challenge to be around Lincoln.

Fiona turned her head and looked at the buildings that she had seen every day and didn't even see them. Her mind was focused on what was she going to do now that Lincoln was going to be a part of her life again. Certainly, this was going to be just a temporary problem. She knew Lincoln. Whatever attraction might be between her and Lincoln, she was going to be able to fight it and move on. After someone has left you once, you shouldn't trust them again, right?

This supposed attraction she felt to Lincoln was nothing more than a test. If anything, it told her she needed to get out more. Some very nice eligible bachelors lived in Rolling Springs. Fiona was sure if she gave them a chance, this whole attraction thing she thought was between her and Lincoln would go away, or at the very least, would fade into the background. With a sigh, she kept walking. This was her world. She knew this block. She knew these buildings. She had the answer to this problem. She was going to live her life as if Lincoln wasn't there.

Six

Lincoln has been standing at the door to Fiona's office for about two minutes. The idea of going inside was giving him more trepidation than facing angry stockholders. He thought yesterday they had gotten off to a pretty good start. Lincoln knew the value of follow-up, and here he was. Standing outside of the door as if this was the first time they were about to go on a date. He had his hand on the door when he saw a movement from the side and turned his head to see a woman approaching him.

"So you must be Lincoln Chase," she said, holding out her hand. Lincoln looked at her hand and had to stop himself from taking a step back. This was not one of his strong suits. The whole touching and physical contact thing wasn't something he was into. In fact, if he was honest, he'd have to say that was one of the main reasons he almost always had Aster with him. No one could see how sweet and gentle Aster was, and as a result, she gave people enough pause that they didn't offer to shake hands. "Hi, I'm Veronica Kaplan. It's nice to finally meet you."

Lincoln just shook his head in agreement. Then they shook hands.

Veronica was probably in her late thirties with short, black curly hair and brown eyes that seemed as though they missed nothing. She was maybe about five foot six, and she had energy about her that made Lincoln nervous.

"Fiona mentioned that you would be coming by to help us out," Veronica said.

"I used to live here, so it's not a big deal for me to help out. And I would like to think that everyone would give help to their hometown if they could."

"I'm sure we would all like to help. However, it's common knowledge that your assistance went above and beyond."

"Money isn't really the important part here," Lincoln said.

She saw her brown eyes sweep him from head to toe, and again he looked around, hoping that somebody would come and save him.

"Forgive me, I'm so rude. I know I Introduced myself, but I forgot to say what it is I actually do. I'm a grant writer, and I'm the one who wrote the grant that brought you here."

All of Lincoln's warning signs went up. You didn't make the kind of money that he did and not run into women who were more interested in the power that surrounded his money or the things that his money could buy. Again, he was beating himself up for not bringing Aster.

"There are a lot of needy projects that are looking for funding," she said. "We are always looking for generous funders in order to help." Veronica smiled. "Maybe we could talk about some of the other opportunities that I could put you in touch with sometime later on…" She paused and smiled wider. "Over dinner."

Fiona could hear everything that was being said. She was inside of her office and was about to go out the door when she saw Lincoln outside. She could see him through the small window that was next to the door. The blinds allowed her to see out without him seeing in. It was that moment of indecision when she saw him outside of the door that had her on this side peeking out the window like some type of voyeur. Just as she was about to open the door, she heard Veronica.

She could tell by looking at Lincoln that he was not happy. After her assumption about him and his money, she could see she wasn't the only one to make those wrong assumptions. Even worse, she could see that some people wanted to take advantage of him because of his money. What made a man leave his offices where he could make thousands or millions within days or even hours and go to a small town like Rolling Springs?

Fiona wasn't one to hide from the truth. She needed to have a very clear and blunt conversation with Lincoln. She needed to understand why he was here and what his intentions were. However, the first thing she needed to do was to save Lincoln. She pulled open the door, and both Lincoln and Veronica turned and looked at her in shock.

Veronica recovered first. "Oh, hello there, Fiona. I was just telling Lincoln how he could help us do so much good in the community."

Fiona glanced over at Lincoln and saw him stiffen as Veronica spoke. She was surprised Veronica couldn't feel the waves of tension coming off of Lincoln.

"You know, I don't want to take up any more of your time, so I'll guess I'll leave you two." Veronica turned toward Lincoln, and she smiled. "Maybe you will think about my offer?"

"I'll see you later, Veronica," Fiona said as Veronica walked away. Fiona saw Lincoln tracking Veronica down the block, looking a lot like his cat Aster, still and calculating.

"So I take it you're not a fan?" Fiona said breaking Lincoln's concentration.

"Not at all."

"It seems like this is going to be our spot. We always seem to meet right here in front of my place. I can see that this was a stressful encounter. Why don't I try to make it up to you by taking you to lunch?"

Lincoln nodded and followed Fiona down the block.

Fiona took them to the same cafe they had passed the last two days. Today was a little different. It wasn't the early morning when it was isolated. Now there were plenty of people in town sitting in the cafe. She ignored the looks that the nearby patrons gave her and concentrated on Lincoln.

When the waitress came to seat them, Lincoln let Fiona lead the way. He waited for her to take a seat at the table before he took his. Fiona couldn't remember the last time someone had shown her those kinds of manners. Or maybe this was just the first time she noticed them. Either way, it didn't matter. What did matter is that she had a chance to get a good look at Lincoln before he took his seat.

He wore black-as-midnight jeans and a button-down shirt. This was the business casual look she'd seen on television, in the office one moment and then going out to a date the next. If he dressed like this all the time, she could definitely see while he was popular. She felt out of place. The only thing she had put on with any care was a sundress, and that was because it was brand new. This morning when she woke up, Fiona wouldn't say that she was dressing for Lincoln, but she did decide that her brand new light blue sundress was something she really wanted to try today. And she had to put on the matching shoes. The sandals were completely impractical for her daily walk.

Not even a week ago, she would have been shaking her head had she seen a woman doing the same thing she's doing now. Fiona never understood how women could send those mixed signals. She never understood until now. She knew the best thing was for her to stay away from Lincoln, but here she was, looking prettier than she had in a while.

She knew her appearance was a shock to the waitress as well. After the waitress had seated them, she saw the young lady look over her shoulder to take a second look at her. When Fiona turned and focused on Lincoln, she second guessed herself. Maybe she was wrong, maybe the young lady hadn't been looking at her, after all.

Once they were settled and seated across from one another, Lincoln gave her a smile that would have stopped a thousand ships. Did the man even know how good he looked when he smiled? It was that dimple. She knew it was that dimple.

"Do you know what you want?" Lincoln asked.

Fiona's first thought was, Of course, I know what I

want. I'm looking at him. Fortunately, her brain was in charge and not her hormones. So instead, she chose a much more mature answer.

"I usually just order the special. It's nothing fancy, just a burger and some fries."

When the waitress approached again, Lincoln didn't even look up at her.

"Please bring us two lunch specials with cola."

Fiona wasn't going to argue with him about ordering for her. Yes, she knew she had told him she typically had the special, but what made him think she still drank cola? She actually still did drink cola, so obviously she was just being contrary. It was time to find out why was Lincoln here.

"You weren't happy with Veronica today," she started wanting to ease into his motives.

"No, but I wasn't surprised by the conversation. I think I was just disappointed."

"Disappointed that she was trying to go on a date with you, or disappointed that she wanted to spend your money?"

Lincoln sighed. "I'd like someone to be able to ask me for something and then let me decide what I'd like to do for them."

Fiona smarted from that answer. "Ouch, it sounds like you have this problem an awful lot."

"I've had my fair share of this issue. I was just hoping that since I was home, I wouldn't have to go through the same thing. I guess I thought that when I came home, people would think they were dealing with the same lonely, isolated teenager. Instead, I came here, and now I find that people are just looking at me as if I'm a dollar bill."

Fiona nodded. "Wow, what makes that so bad is I was in the same boat with the rest of them. It's hard to imagine that someone who has left rolling Springs and who is so well-known and so successful doesn't have the perfect life."

Lincoln shifted in his chair. "Of course, of course, my life must be perfect because everyone sees every aspect of it and understands that there is nothing wrong anywhere. You know, it doesn't really matter. I'll probably give Veronica a call later, and I'll see which one of the projects she wants me to do."

"Why?"

"Why what?"

"Why do it if you really don't want to?"

The waitress came and placed their sodas in front of the both of them before walking away.

"Fiona, I'm doing the best that I can do. I want to be able to help everyone out, but as soon as I got here, all of my plans were marked up and changed. I don't want to be the guy who thinks he can tell everybody what to do because he has money. I'm trying to do the right thing here, and at the same time not to go over everything just because I'm signing the check."

"I think the idea is noble, Lincoln. But you have to be careful that you don't let your money pick your friends. If you don't want to do a project that Veronica suggests, then don't do it. If you never say no to anyone, they will always expect you to say yes."

Lincoln stopped and stared at her. She waited, hoping he would take a sip of his soda or something. It was a second before she was ready to shift in her seat to see that he sat back.

"Tell me, Fiona, what would you think if I said no to something?"

"Me? I know I don't think this is really about me. But I will answer your question. I don't expect you to say yes to everything that I say. I understand that you and I are different people, and if you said yes to everything, then I would think you were patronizing me."

He grabbed the glass and took a sip. Fiona would have thought as picky as he was that he would use a straw, but that didn't happen. Instead, something that should have been boring became an event. His hands were strong as they wrapped around the glass. He had no scratches, no marks. Instead, he had the long fingers of a pianist. When he lifted the glass up to drink, he didn't pause. What was wrong with her? When did watching someone drink cola become a sexy commercial moment?

Like a child that had been caught peeking around the corner as soon as he put his cuff down, she grabbed her drink and gulped down her soda.

"I'll ask Veronica to send over a proposal. Then what I can do is see what the goals are, and I can ask my friends if they're interested.

"Thank you."

"Too easy, Lincoln, that issue was just too easy."

The food was brought to the table, and after a couple of things Lincoln looked as though he was genuinely enjoying himself.

"So I take it you like the special?" Fiona said as she ate her fries.

"What was your hint? Maybe the way I totally demolished this burger. it was a new experience for me, eating lunch without Aster."

"Is she always with you?"

"Let's just say I happen to prefer her company to most people."

Fiona heard Lincoln say the words, and for a moment she understood, but it was like to have people around you but to still be alone. It seemed as though neither one of them had been able to find someone who could understand them and stay around them. Lincoln had his cat and his money. She had the town and her father. It looked like time had not been kind to either one of them when it came to love and they both had the scars to prove it.

Lincoln explained to Fiona how he had made money creating algorithms. They finished eating their lunch, arguing about who was really in charge, Irma or Dione. A principal versus a librarian seemed to be a very equal match.

When the table was finally cleared, Fiona stood up. "If you need help facing the two of them, you know you can always call on me."

"I'm so glad that you extended the offer. Does that offer include your phone number?"

Fiona hesitated for a moment, and then she gave him her number. It was just to get the town the help they needed. While those were the words her brain was saying, her heart was skipping a beat and doing flips, and all of a sudden there was a smile trying to slip out.

He held his hand out and walked her to the sidewalk. Again, they found themselves where they had been for the last three mornings in front of what was now becoming their spot.

"Well, I've got to be going back to work. But I just have to ask you one question," she said.

"Go for it."

"We have been talking this whole afternoon about what you can do for Rolling Springs, and I want you to know I'm so grateful that you are doing the grant application and being so generous to the town. What keeps rolling around in the back of my head that I don't have an answer for is why?"

"Why what, Fiona?"

"Why are you doing this? You were always a logical person, and you never did anything without a reason. Not to say that you were manipulative or anything. I'm just saying you're a big boy now, and you are in control of a lot of money. There are a lot of towns out there. Why rolling Springs, and why now?"

He took a step toward her and leaned in until she could feel his breath on her ear lobe.

"I came back for the most priceless thing in Rolling Spring. You, Fiona Dunn. The reason I came home was for you." Then, as she stood stock still unable to believe the words whispered in her ear, he placed a kiss on her cheek.

He stepped back and smiled at her.

"Thanks for an amazing lunch." And then he walked away.

Fiona stood on the sidewalk and watched him walk away, star struck. Her body was in overdrive. Her mind was trying to talk some common sense to the rest of her hormones, and all in all, it made her stand there unsure what to do. There was no denying it now, she was still attracted to Lincoln, and it wasn't going away.

It was time to call reinforcements because she couldn't trust her judgment when it came to Lincoln.

Seven

There was only one other diner in Rolling Springs, and it was called The Flagship. Later that evening, Fiona found herself sitting in The Flagship waiting for her best friend Sherry Marksman.

"I'm here. I canceled all of my evening classes. I figured if you asked me to come out this time of night, it must be serious."

Fiona watched her best friend slip into the booth. Today she had on one of her pixie wigs. It was bronze and blonde. Fiona had stopped trying to keep track of what new hairstyle Sherry would have on today.

"Thanks for coming on such short notice," Fiona told her friend. Sherry stopped and gave Fiona a long look.

"This must be something really serious," Sherry said.

"The end of the world does not have to be happening for me to call you."

"Maybe not the end of the world, but it's got to be something real close. As a professional in choosing Mr. Wrong, I can only guess that this has something to do with a man."

Fiona knew this was a double-edged sword. On the one hand, she knew there wasn't anything sure he wouldn't do for her, but he would come with Sherry's own personal comments about how everything should have been done in the first place.

Fiona admired Sherry. She knew Sherry thought every time she picked a guy and he turned out to be the wrong one, Sherry felt that she just had the worst luck in the world. But when Fiona looked at Sherry she saw an amazingly strong and courageous woman who was willing to try and try again in order to find that one true love. Maybe if she knew how to do that, she wouldn't be in this situation. Perhaps, if she hadn't already decided on who that one true love was, she could have found someone else.

Sherry reached across the table and placed her hand on atop of Fiona's.

"Hey, Fiona, you know no matter what it is, I've got your back."

Fiona nodded. "I needed to call you because Lincoln is back in town."

Fiona expected Sherry to say something right away. Instead, Sherry just sat back and waited.

"Aren't you going to say something?"

"Well, I'm not really sure what you want me to say. Rolling Springs is a very small town. He could walk right through this town and not even know it. On top of that, I know he's giving some money in order to build the center. It seems like a very trendy thing to do with all those people who have lots of money. It's a way for them to remember where they came from, or to show others they remember where they came from. Why does it matter?"

"It matters because I have to work with him." Fiona didn't understand why she was acting like this. Maybe she had made a mistake in calling Sherry?

"The only reason it would matter is if you still had feelings for him. But we've had this conversation, and every time I bring it up, you always tell me, 'No, no, no, that ship has passed. I don't feel anything for him.' Would you like to tell me what's going on now between you and Lincoln?"

"That is the question, isn't it? If you had asked me two weeks ago, I would have laughed and told you nothing was going on. Because even if he's giving the money for the town, I don't feel anything for him. Now? I'm not so sure."

"Not that I have been listening, mind you, but I can tell you that Lincoln has been telling people around town he thinks the improvements are well done. He hasn't hesitated to praise you for taking care of issues when no one else would."

The waitress came and set down two glasses of water. Fiona didn't know what to say. Hearing that Lincoln was talking about her and singing her praises made her back straighten a little bit. Realizing that he recognized what she did caused heat waves to radiate from her core. It warmed her and made her smile at the same time.

"Oh my goodness, are you sitting over there with the 'I've got a secret. I know that someone loves me but no one else knows' look?"

"No!" Fiona's head popped up from her water, and she gave Sherry a stoic look. "I told you we are helping each other out while we're trying to get this project done.

We've been meeting in the mornings, but that's only because he has a cat and I do the daily walkthrough."

Sherry leaned back into the booth and smiled.

"Wow, it's been a long time since you tried to skirt around the truth with me."

"I'm not skirting."

"So you still think he is the underside of a snake's belly?"

"Did I say that?"

Sherry smiled even wider. "You said that and so much more."

Fiona moved the glass of water to the side and dropped her head into her hands on top of the table.

"What was I thinking, and what am I doing?"

"That Lincoln looks amazing. You might be doing what every other woman in this town would like to do. You might just be getting to know him. Is that a problem?"

Fiona groaned. "Yes, it is a problem."

Sherry placed her elbow on top of the table and leaned to one side. "This, I've got to hear."

"You know that Lincoln and I both have history. The problem is, he's not the same Lincoln I knew."

"I hope not. You aren't children anymore. This isn't high school. That's a great thing, no?"

"It's a great thing, and it isn't. I'm not sure what I'm doing, and when I asked him why he's here, let's just say, his answer wasn't what I was expecting."

"If it's any consolation, you two still make an adorable couple."

"No, it's no consolation at all."

Sherry laughed. "Remember, you call me because I'm not your logical head that has to have a reason for everything. I'm your friend, and most importantly,

I'm not afraid of you. I'm here to determine the best thing for my friend. Right now, the way you light up when you talk about him, the way you're dressing, and your smile leads me to say the best thing for you is Lincoln Chase."

"If I listen to you, I'll end up dating him, and that is so not going to happen. Not until I get some things cleared up with myself and with him.

Eight

"These requests can't be for real," Lincoln said, looking at the documentation before him.

"Now, now, you're just hoping they aren't for real, but you already know the truth. Each one was thought out and vetted before they were put into the plan," Fiona said.

Today Lincoln had decided it would be a good time for the both of them to go over the different conditions that were put into the project.

"Honestly, I can't see why this is such a big deal to you. It's my understanding you make your living wheeling and dealing with people all the time. Certainly you're not saying that two senior women are going to get the best of you?"

"These are more than just two senior women. They bring with them the full force of their principal and their library and knowledge in order to twist a little boy into making him do what they want him to do."

"Are you trying to say you're still a little boy?"

"When they walk into the room. I have no shame. Yes, I am."

Fiona laughed. "I guess what they say is true. That coming home can humble of man."

He shuffled some of the papers on the table and then tried to put them in some kind of order. Instead, he just shook his head and put them all down. "Humble a man? This is way more than humbling a man. To think that once upon a time I used to go to my work in order to find some peace and solace."

"Okay, now I even feel sorry for you. Why don't we take a break?"

Today, Lincoln had made it past the front door, and they were in one of the two rooms of Fiona's office. When she suggested that they take a break, she stood up and pointed toward the open door to her left. "I've got a makeshift kitchen in there. We can go and get some coffee."

Lincoln followed her into the kitchen. When she had called her earlier, he wanted to go over the conditions in the project. After they had assessed them, there was definitely more than ten mandatory modifications. As a result, Fiona suggested that he come by and they could work on them together.

"Take a seat. How do you want your coffee?" Fiona asked.

"Black. Maybe it will throw off some of the haze."

Fiona delivered the two piping cups of coffee as they stood around the island in the kitchen.

"Okay you have to tell me what is the problem. Like I said before, I can't imagine anything they put in the project that you haven't seen before."

"You see, that's where you are wrong. It's like one declaration says they want to make sure the workers in the center get lunch. No problem. I was planning to give them lunch. Then the document says they don't start lunch until their food arrives on the table. Okay it means I say take lunch. Then there is another subsection that says that if the person is over the age of sixty, I have to provide those lunches as well, and that is one example of the issue.

I want to build in an equitable platform for people, but some of the requests go above and beyond."

Fiona nodded, and then they walked back to the working table. With coffee cups cradled in their hands, they went back to the work table. Fiona looked at the work on the table.

"Is there anything you can't do, or would be so cost prohibitive that you would have to say no to the project?"

"No, it just doesn't make a lot of sense money wise."

"They want all they can get, and I know it won't be easy to pick and choose."

"It's part of my plan. I want the town to be comfortable with me."

She nodded in agreement. "I didn't appreciate until very recently how hard this must be for you. Like I said before, I was a part of those people who judged you."

"That's true, but that was also before you understood why I'm actually back in town."

So there it was, the elephant in the room. Fiona was hoping that pseudo-confession was just an aberration. Now that he was bringing it up again, it must not be.

"Lincoln, I want you to know I understand how people say things, and they are just—"

Lincoln put his coffee cup aside. Then he moved her cup and placed his hands over hers.

"Fiona, don't try to sweep it away. Let me tell you

this. I meant what I said. I need to know how you feel about it."

"You want to come back to podunk USA? You have to understand how odd that sounds. Then, when I ask you why you say—"

He grinned. "Because the most amazing woman ever born lives here. I say I'm coming back because I realized, no matter how far I go, you are the one steady factor in my life. I'm just tired of checking up on you from afar. Yes. I'm coming back to podunk USA for you."

"Your friends—"

"You met my best friend, and she loved you, Aster."

"Lincoln?"

"Why the hesitation, Fiona? Am I repulsive to you, or is your heart with someone else?"

Fiona shook her head. "No, no, it's nothing like that, at all. I think I just need some time. Why don't we put this part off until tomorrow? I need to clear my thoughts and my head."

Lincoln smiled and nodded. He stood up, and Fiona followed him to the door. She was numb, and looking at him didn't help him.

"Stop worrying, Fiona. Remember, it's my job to plan and work things out. Whatever you think is a big issue, probably isn't. If there is an issue, between your brain and my money, I think we can solve it. I'll see you tomorrow at your place. Is that okay?"

She nodded.

Then he reached out and lifted her chin so her eyes were looking directly into his. She saw his head coming down, and as he got closer, she felt sparks go off around her belly button. When his lips touched hers, it was a balm to ease the slow burn that had been building up within her. When his lips left, she followed, and she heard her name murmured against her lips.

She opened her eyes and found Lincoln gazing down at her with such adoration, she had to look away from the intensity. He stepped away.

"Until tomorrow." Then he was gone.

Fiona looked at the door and closed her eyes, and the wave of need and warmth went through her.

"I've got to tell him," she murmured and then wrapped her arms around herself, trying to savor what could have been the last time she would ever feel Lincoln's arms around her.

Nine

Lincoln had to admit he had contemplated bringing Aster. Today was going to be so important. He was willing to use anything he had in his arsenal to ensure it all went well. Going to Fiona's house could be an obstacle. Rolling Springs was a very small town. When she gave him her address, and he'd thought it was the house where she had grown up. As he drove down the road, he found that she was a half-mile away from the old farm where she used to live.

When he pulled up into the dirt road, he wasn't surprised at what he found. Fiona loved flowers. It looked like the property had been a small farm. A family who'd had two cows at best. She had taken that house and made it into a cozy cottage.

The cottage was straight out of the conversations they had talked about as children. There were two rectangular lawns in front of the home. On the right, was a small little pond, circled by flowers of different heights. On the left, were vegetables planted along the fence, but in the middle was grass and a little picnic table with a small barbecue grill behind it.

Looking at the house brought a smile to Lincoln's face. It was nice to know there were some things that she had kept from her childhood. He was banking on the idea that he was going to be one of those things as well. He walked up the path, and before he reached his hand to the door, it opened.

Fiona looked frazzled.

"It was so silly of me. I didn't even give you the complete address. I just told you half a mile away from the old place. What was I thinking? Like you would remember anything about this place."

She opened the door and stepped to the side as she rattled on. As Lincoln walked into the home, he could almost feel the waves of anxiety and tension coming off of her. There were little telltale signs about Fiona that always told him when something was wrong. It was the way that she had a ponytail tied back but it was a bit crooked and leaned to the left. It was the fact that she had on her yoga pants and a sleeveless running top. Those were the clothes that she wore right before she did a run to work off some excess energy. He used to tease her when they were kids, saying if she wanted to work off excess energy she could always solve a problem. She would always joke that it was easier to run.

"Are you sure you want me to be here?" he asked.

"Yes, yes. I'm sure. Well, I mean, it doesn't really matter. It's not like it will change anything, and what must be done has to be done. So please, come in and take a seat."

Lincoln looked around at the oversized furniture in the room. Again, it was just as they had dreamed about when they were kids. Lincoln used to always complain that his mother had the prettiest, most delicate furniture there was. If a person weighed more than a hundred pounds, they would break every piece of furniture in his mom's living room. Together they had made a promise that if they ever bought living room furniture, it would be oversized pieces that you could lay on, go to sleep on, or do whatever you want.

He sat on the loveseat. The chair was plush and soft and he slowly sank into it with no problem. It didn't surprise him that the furniture was upholstered in bold floral prints of blue and beige. The colors matched the beige shades and the window treatments that had Blue Jays and dandelions with sheer white accent curtains underneath. Straight ahead was a hallway that led further back into the house. When he looked to his left he could see an arched doorway that appeared to go to the kitchen.

As he was taking in his surroundings, Fiona took a seat on the far end of the love seat. Lincoln was concerned that if was she moved any further to the end she would fall off onto the floor.

"Fiona?"

Fiona held up her hand and stopped him from talking.

"I want you to know that I heard you, and I understood what you said to me yesterday. But before you commit to staying here because of me, I want to clear the air."

"Clear the air?"

"Yes, I have to do this," she said as she wrung her hands together in her lap. "I thought this would be so much easier than what it's turning out to be. It's not like either one of us could fix this."

Lincoln was on edge. "Fiona, tell me. Whatever it is, we can fix it."

Fiona's eyes began to water, and she shook her head slowly. "Lincoln, some things can't be fixed. Sometimes there are things we have to live with or they will eat us up from the inside." She stood up and paced right to left, then she came back to the side of the loveseat, crossed arms over her chest, and let out a massive sigh.

Lincoln was tensed and ready for anything. He wanted to grab her and hold her in his arms, but he knew Fiona. She'd want to speak her mind and wouldn't appreciate him treating her like a child. It was one of the things he loved about her. She was independent to the end.

"I thought about what you said. About being in Rolling Springs for me."

"Yes, I am here because of you. Because I—"

Fiona held up her hand and stopped his speech. "Listen first," she said. She walked over to him and placed her hand on his cheek, then traced her fingers down his jaw to his chin, before letting her hand fall away.

"We need to talk about the night you left."

"The night I left?" he asked, confused. "I don't think I would have used those words, but okay."

Fiona sat back down. "The night you left, my father came to me and told me you were going on to bigger and better things. He told me I wasn't smart enough to be with you, and that you had finally come to your senses."

Lincoln felt as if he had been punched to his gut. The air went out of him, and his jaw tightened. "He lied," he said flatly.

Fiona nodded. "It wasn't like you to just leave. We always talked about everything, so when he told me you had left, I knew something was wrong." She drew in a shaky breath and continued, "It didn't take long before my father confessed what he had done. He said he told you I was ashamed of you, and that was why we never met in public. He said you were going to go off, and maybe you'd do something, maybe you wouldn't. But he had bigger and better plans for me, and that I couldn't follow you. Nothing he said mattered. I told him I was still going to pack my bags at the end of the semester, which was just in a couple of days anyway, and I'd go find you. Then he told me he'd been diagnosed with cancer. He said, if I left, it would be a death sentence for him."

Lincoln knew he was not a man prone to violence. But in that moment all he wanted to do was rage and scream and somehow take all of this anger and hurt that had been inflicted upon them both and make someone else pay.

He realized that, at the end of the day, he was still Fiona's father. He had to keep himself together and to pull his composure, from where, he didn't know, but this he could do for Fiona. She didn't need to see his anger and anguish at the man.

"How is he?" It seemed so bland and disingenuous.

"He lied."

"Excuse me?"

"My father knew someone who had cancer, and he would go with them to the doctor appointments. He never wanted me to go because he said he didn't want me to see him in pain. He took those forms and my father put his name on them and we went on like that for about three months."

"Is he still alive?"

She nodded. "I see him almost every day."

"You see him…" Lincoln echoed the words, not sure he could really process any more.

"I wanted this to be clear between us. I wanted to tell you this because I know what he did was wrong. I know he believed he did it for all of the right reasons, and still, it doesn't make it any more right," she said, staring at him. "More importantly if you're really going to be here for me you'd have to understand he's still a part of my life."

Lincoln swallowed and tried to digest the words she was saying. The man who had stolen so much time from them was here. He was walking about as if nothing was wrong. The man that had made Fiona suffer as much as him hadn't paid the price for what he had done.

"How do you do it? How do you see him every day?"

"I do it because I can't change it. I do it because he's my father. He was doing what he thought was best."

"Are you trying to convince me or yourself?"

"We both have to believe it if we're going to have a chance to be together." Fiona swallowed. "I want to be with you, Lincoln. I want to see if what we had is still there. But I want to make sure we start on the right foot and everything is out in the open. You need to decide if you can get past this or not."

Lincoln stood up he looked around the room and then back and Fiona. "I need time to put this all together in my head," he said.

"I understand."

Lincoln nodded and then he left out the front door. When he got outside he couldn't even tell what was to the right or to the left of him. Lincoln had no idea what he was going to do or how it was going to work out. The feeling was uncomfortable and scary all at the same time.

Ten

Lincoln tried to lose himself in the everyday hustle and bustle of his life. He had already opened his emails and finished his morning workout. After that, he couldn't even take Aster for a walk. He had set up a desk with two curved screens on it so he could monitor the activity in his company and his investments.

Life in Rolling Springs was different. Had he been home in New York, he would have walked the streets, surrounded by the digital output of the market and the constant chatter of people moving and cars rushing. Back in the city, they would have started at six so he could see what had happened on the international markets the day before and would have ended at four-thirty, the close of the market for the day. Between watching the market all day, figuring out problems, and answering emails, Lincoln had a full life. There was little to none of that activity in Rolling Springs.

The issue with living in Rolling Springs was the lack of decent housing. He was living about a mile away from Fiona in a renovated farmhouse. At the time, it seemed rustic when the realtor showed it to him.

But he had chosen this house because it used to be his. If he was going to come back to Rolling Springs, then he was going to go all the way back. The house reminded him of his humble beginnings. He had someone come in and make some changes to it, so while the exterior may have looked like a farmhouse, the interior could compete with the best lofts in New York City.

Along the walls were staggered shelves that weren't really shelves but ledges for Aster to jump on. Making sure that Aster had a cattery built-in was just as important to him as making sure he had an internet connection.

He looked around at the circular sofa and the theater screen on the wall. He knew it was sparse, but he didn't want to put too much into the place because he was waiting for Fiona to come and make it theirs.

He sat back in his chair at his desk and leaned his head against the headrest, letting his mind wander. He had to think about him and Fiona. Somehow, he had to figure out what he wanted to do about Fiona's dad.

He thought about when he first met Fiona, back in eighth grade. He'd been in the gifted classes, and one day, he decided to leave his class and see how the other eighth graders lived.

But when he went to the classroom, everyone was gone to lunch. He was about to leave when he heard the sound of chalk on the chalk board. He stepped further into the class and saw a girl writing on the board. Upon further inspection, he saw what she was writing: I will not disturb the class.

Lincoln made some noise, and the girl whipped around. Her ponytail was so long it swung and hit her forehead. She rubbed her forehead and then looked at him with her wide brown eyes.

"You're not in the right class. This class is at lunch, so why are you here? And who are you?"

"I'm Lincoln Chase. You're right, this isn't my class. Why are you writing that on the board?"

The girl looked around and then sat down in the nearby chair.

"My name is Fiona Dunn. I said something in class, and the teacher didn't like it."

"What did you say?"

She shrugged. "I told her the fact that she can tell me what to do and how to do it at my desk suggests that I'm living with imperialism in the classroom. It didn't seem fair since every day we said it was a democracy in the classroom and we should vote on everything. I asked her if we could vote about this as well. She was not happy."

Lincoln smiled. When she smiled back at him, he had known. And as they dated through the years, it only became more apparent she was the one. He had thought about everything he wanted to do with his life, and how he wanted Fiona to be a part of it.

After her father sent him away, his world had been forever changed. As time has gone on he had learned how to survive, but he didn't really live. With every new experience he wondered what Fiona would think. He had dated. He had met other women who were amazing. But the heart can't be reasoned with. The one thing his heart wanted was Fiona.

Lincoln liked Fiona as a person. He loved the way she stood up for what she believed in, even when it wasn't popular. Lincoln wanted to be able to go to her and to say they could work through this problem with her father. Maybe if they didn't have to see him every day he could do it, but—

People came to him all the time to solve problems. He always told people to think about the goal and not necessarily the obstacles. He was being given a second chance with Fiona. The goal was to be with the one woman he truly loved. He needed Fiona. If there was going to be a chance for him to really care about someone, to really know what it was like to love and truly be loved by someone other than Aster,. he was going to have to make some hard decisions. Maybe Fiona wasn't the only one who had some confessions to make. If he were honest, he would admit it tore them apart when they allowed their insecurities to rule them. At any time, either one of them could have called the other and cleared it all up, but the words that Fiona's father had spoken had a hint of truth for each of them, and that hint of truth was enough to stop them both. Maybe this time they could find a way to not just love each other but to trust each other.

Maybe?

"Okay, I'll admit that I'm intrigued," Sherry said as she closed the door to Fiona's office. She had the kind of smile that made Fiona nervous, but Sherry was her best friend. "I've once again put those eager homebound kiddie minds on pause so I could come and attend to your delicate issues."

Fiona rolled her eyes. She knew what she was getting into with Sherry but she needed her bestie, even if that bestie was a little extra sometimes.

"You want coffee? I called because I need you."

Sherry's whole demeanor changed.

"You know whatever you need I'm here for you."

Fiona almost cried when she heard that. She hid her tears by blinking her eyes and getting some coffee for Sherry. Fiona didn't know what she was going to do. Having Sherry come to help her out was something she needed even more than she knew.

"I've got a problem."

"Does the problem have brown eyes and an incredible build with a hot look?"

Fiona smiled. Sherry knew everything there was to know about her and Lincoln. Sherry had been with Fiona since the beginning. When she had broken up with Lincoln, Sherry was the one who said run out to him and go and talk to him. It wasn't what she wanted to hear at the time and she definitely didn't want to hear that her father would do anything wrong.

"Yes the problem is Lincoln."

"I think I also told you the problem wasn't just Lincoln. If we really look at this the problem is about trust."

"Trust. It always comes back to that, doesn't it?" Fiona said. Fiona wanted to get up and pace and somehow burn off this extra energy that she seemed to have. "You're right, it is about trust, and here I am and here is Lincoln. What am I going to do?"

Sherry held up her hands and shook her head. "I hope you didn't invite me here so that I could tell you what to do so you can say you had no responsibility over the end result? If so, one of us is about to be seriously disappointed."

Fiona swallowed and then sat back in her chair. "I'm not looking for a scapegoat. I told Lincoln everything."

Sherry sat back and looked at Fiona with eyes wide

open. Sherry's hand came up to cover her mouth as if she was in shock.

"You told him everything everything?"

"Yes."

"Mister   I've-got-entirely-too-much-money-with-a-really-cool-cat? You told him everything?"

Fiona nodded again. "I had to do something. I finally confronted him and asked him why he was here."

Sherry leaned in closer to Fiona. "And?"

"And he said he was here for me. Can you imagine him saying that to me? How could I not tell him the truth?"

"It seems like you've already let the cat out the bag. Why am I here?"

"You are here because I told him two days ago. He said he needed some time. I think I made a mistake and maybe telling him was the worst thing ever."

"Listen to me. Fiona. You are one of the good guys," Sherry said. "You make the hard decisions and the tough calls. I can see how you might be second guessing yourself, so if you called me so I could confirm that you did the right thing, the answer is, yes, you did."

Fiona sighed. "Knowing I did the right thing doesn't make me feel any better when I think it might have cost me the man of a lifetime."

Sherry smiled. "Personally, I think you're thinking about this all wrong. You know what the potential problem is and you know what the outcomes are. The only thing you need to do is plan for both outcomes."

"How does one plan for rejection?"

"You plan on not accepting that outcome. If he makes the wrong decision, you have to change his mind, but Lincoln seems like a smart guy. I don't think he's going to reject you." Sherry's expression softened. "Remember what I said, this whole situation is about trust. Trust in yourself, and then you two can trust in each other."

"The last time I trusted a man he betrayed me. How do I get past my fear that my judgment isn't all that good?"

"I can see you would worry yourself into a rabbit hole, so this is going to be my advice for you. Don't borrow trouble until it gets here."

"That's it!"

"Hey, don't knock it until you've tried it. Now enough of this maudlin conversation about doom, gloom, and rejection. I think what you should do, in order to pick your spirits up, is to take a friend out to lunch. Fortunately for you, my afternoon is clear."

They stood up, and Fiona went to Sherry and hugged her.

"Thanks for coming," Fiona whispered.

"Of course, besides who doesn't go to see the sequel of a great romance?"

Sherry pulled back and smiled. "Come on, let's see if I can find a hot dog stand for you."

Eleven

Fiona was on pins and needles the whole time. She had called Sherry at least five times over the last couple of days. She was surprised that Sherry hadn't blocked her phone number. Since then she had tried to re-create the curriculum she planned to submit to the council for review. After she had put in the curriculum and double checked her email for an approval from them she was left with herself and her thoughts.

Fiona wasn't a particular fan of waiting for anything. She didn't like waiting for Christmas presents. Fiona didn't like surprises and she surely didn't like waiting for Lincoln. She was at the office working on numbers when she had added the same column five times and decided that she needed to walk away or next time she'd imagine a new number just to add something else in the mix. Just as she was about to stand up, the door opened.

Lincoln stood at the door and he had Aster with him. Her heart quickened as she looked at him unsure of what he was going to say. Had he brought Aster to protect him when he said that he wouldn't be able to deal with her and her father?

"Yes?" she said in a tone sterner than she had meant it to be. She wanted to hit herself over the head. What if he had come to say yes? If that was the case, then she had just snapped at the man she had been waiting for all of her life.

Lincoln closed the door and let the leash fall out of his hand.

"I don't know what is on that paper but whatever it is I apologize for it," he said. His comment made her look down at her hand and she could see she had a death grip on the pencil, and the lead was being crushed.

"My mind is elsewhere."

"I was hoping that it was the document."

She let out a deep sigh. "I've been waiting for an answer from some man and I find that trying to do work while I'm waiting on something is not conducive to me being productive."

"Oh."

"Oh? Is that all you have to say Lincoln Chase? I hope you've come to give me more than that!"

She thought about getting up and offering him something, but why? This was her office, and she needed answers. Just as she was about to tear into him again, her vision was obstructed by Aster. She was humongous! Fiona hadn't really appreciated how big Aster was. Aster arched her back and then turned to give Fiona a lick on her face.

"Yeah, she really likes you," Lincoln said.

Fiona wanted to say who cares but just then she put her hand out to stop Aster's bushy tail from hitting her in the face and she fell in love. Aster's fur felt soft as silk. Fiona wound up putting her hands in Aster's fur and stroking the cats back until she got a purr out of her.

It was the most incredible experience she had ever had with an animal. It became all the more special when she realized her hands were going over corded muscles in Aster and that while Aster looked cute and fluffy, she could do some real damage.

"I really like her too, Lincoln. She feels amazing!" Fiona said.

She didn't hear Lincoln take a seat. Fiona saw his arms wrap around Aster and put her on the floor and then she was facing him across the table.

Lincoln looked amused almost. "You get a little crabby when things aren't going your way, don't you?"

She joined in the fun. "Maybe?

She turned away and reached down to pet Aster. After getting her composure she then looked back at Lincoln. She had left one hand on the table. Lincoln's hand was next to hers. Even their hands seemed to say that they were living a different life. Her nails were cracked and uneven. His nails were manicured, buffed and even.

As she was looking at their hand he placed his on top of hers.

"Can we do this, Fiona?"

His voice pulled her in. It was as if he could cast a spell with his voice. The warmth from his hand seemed to seep into hers. She wondered if their relationship would be this easy. If she just had to say yes and they could find a way.

Sherry's words came back to her. She was older now. She understood that what this was really about was trust. She took a deep breath and then looked into his eyes.

"Yes, we can try this."

Lincoln laughed." I'm glad you said that because for a moment there I wasn't sure which way it was going to go."

The statement made her feel better, like she wasn't the only one who was unsure.

"I don't believe in leaving things to chance, Fiona, so tell me tell me about you and your father? It's going to come up sometime and I think we should deal with it sooner rather than later."

She mentally shuddered. "You want to talk about my father?"

"I didn't say that, although I'm sure that's what's about to happen. I really want to know about your whole family. We never went to each other's houses so we never saw that side of each other. What about your mother, and then we can talk about your dad."

"My mother? That is an interesting question. I'm probably not the best person to get the accounting from, but my mother left before I was six. The memories I have of her are few. The ones I do recall were happy. The memories I have are just of me and my mother, never all three of us."

"Did you ever think about looking for her?"

Fiona gave a sad smile. "I took my father at his word and for a very long time I was just so angry. So angry that I didn't want to find her. When I got older, I thought it was too late to find her."

"So why are you willing to give this a chance?"

Lincoln smiled, then he picked up the leash that he had left on the floor and called after Aster so he could put her back on it. When he stood up, he wiped some invisible hair from his jeans and then gazed into Fiona's eyes.

"I told you before you are the one. You are a lot like Aster here. She's a Maine Coon cat and she's opinionated and can't be trusted in public. At least, that's what the documentation says. I even had a vet tell me I should get her declawed as a safety measure for the public. I wouldn't change a thing about Aster. She is unique, beautiful in her own right, and one of a kind. You are one of a kind, my first and only love, Fiona. So yeah, I'm willing to give it a go."

Fiona felt her hand go to her chest. In and out, that was the way to breathe. In and out. The world was tilting on its access, and there was a burst of warmth in her body that gave new meaning to the words 'hot flash'.

"I'm not the same malleable girl that you left, you know. You'll probably get tired of me."

"Don't worry, I'm not the same boy who was here before either. Stop stalling on the other side of that desk. I'm waiting for my kiss to see me off."

She hadn't heard those words since he left. When they had first started meeting in secret, at the end of every meet, she would tell him, let me give you a kiss to see you off. He always said it sounded so ominous, like he wasn't going to come back. She told him the kiss was to make sure that he did. She had to blink back the tears that threatened to fall from her eyes and swallow past the lump that had formed in her throat. He remembered.

She walked around the desk and stood on the other side of Aster.

"If you think the space is going to deter me, you have a lot to learn about me."

Then Lincoln leaned over reached out to tilt her chin up, then pressed his lips to hers lightly. He brushed her lips once, then he brushed by them again. When she saw him angle his head to the side, she was sure he was going to brush by one more time, but instead, he whispered, "I'll always come back, but thank you for the incentive."

Lincoln stood up and walked toward the door. Fiona watched the door close, and her hand went to her lips. She was in so much trouble. This new Lincoln might be more than she could handle. Despite that thought, a little part of her was excited to be here. Walking back to her desk, she decided she would call it a day. She scooped up her papers with a smile and headed toward the door. Just before she got to the door, a knock sounded. She looked up at the clock on the wall and knew who was on the other side.

She could feel her body tense from head to toe as if it were in a vice. A pressure suddenly suffused her head, like she had a migraine coming. For one inexplicable moment, she wondered where she could hide in the room. Then her father stepped into the room and said the words that she knew would be nothing but despair.

"Was that the Chase boy that just left here with a cat?"

Twelve

"Fiona Ann, are you going to answer me?"

What was it about parents calling you by your full name that put everyone on edge?

"Dad."

Connor Dunn closed the door and stood in front of it with his arms crossed over his barrel-sized chest. He was about six foot even and even at seventy-one, he was still an impressive man to look at. Sure, his hair had greyed, and it was a little thinner than before but he still kept it stylish. Her dad had taken to combing his hair one side.

Fiona acknowledged that she had inherited her looks from her mother but she had gotten her inner strength from her father. As a child her dad had left her with women to watch her as he went from one job to the next. On weekends they always drove to a museum or to some educational place. He never missed a weekend. They went to the movies every Wednesday night, even if he went to sleep midway through most movies. She knew he adored and loved her, and as time went on, it seemed that was part of the problem.

Her father stood as if he were guarding the door, but she was pretty sure it was to keep her in. She had always felt small and protected around her dad but lately she was starting to feel like he was Goliath and she was David.

"Well aren't you going to answer me?"

"I'm sorry, I wasn't sure you wanted an answer. Or you were waiting for me to cower?" Fiona threw back her shoulder and went to her father and hugged him. She kissed him on the cheek and then took a step back.

"So was that the Chase boy?"

"He's not a boy, and yes it was. Can you tell me why you came by today? It's not our day to meet."

"Oh so I can only come on special days?"

"No, you can see me whenever you want but I have to think something is different if you are breaking a habit that you've kept for the last fifteen years."

Connor opened his arms and softened his gaze. "You can't blame me for being concerned."

Fiona had to hold her tongue. Actually, she could blame him but she had put that away.

"What about the Chase boy?" he asked, pointing over his shoulder at the door.

Fiona looked around her dad and shrugged. "It seems like he left."

"I see that you've taken a little more care about what you have on today," her father said.

Fiona looked at her clothes and then looked at her father. She shook her head and sighed.

"I didn't dress for him if that's where you're going with this."

Her father held his hands up in defense.

"I'm not saying that, I'm just noticing."

Fiona laughed. "You are so funny, Dad. You've never noticed what I had on. I think as long as I have clothing on over the important sections of my body you've been fine."

Connor's jaw clenched. "I don't think that's really true Fifi. I notice everything about you."

"It's Fiona."

"I know your name, Fifi."

"Why is it the only time you say my first name is when you say my second name and I'm in trouble? All of the other times, you call me Fifi which drives me crazy because it sounds like the name that goes to a little white poodle."

"There is nothing wrong with a father having a nickname for his daughter."

"That might be true, but the problem here is you don't like my first name because Mom gave it to me."

Fiona threw her hands up in the air and turned around to take the seat at her desk. They had had this fight so many times before. It was always the same. She didn't even know why she tried with him anymore. Her father was set in his ways. If it wasn't about him and it wasn't about what they did together, he didn't want her to talk about it at all. All Connor Dunn wanted from his daughter Fiona was for her to be completely happy with him and him alone.

"I can see you're getting stubborn," her father said.

Fiona looked away at the floor and saw a hairball roll across it. She had to remember that even though her father loved her he still would do anything to keep her with him.

"Okay, so you came over because you heard Lincoln was in town."

Her father walked over to the table and pulled out the seat Lincoln had just been sitting in. "You always think I have an ulterior motive."

"Because you usually do have one," Fiona put her hands on top of the table and then let out a deep breath. "Okay I'll give you the benefit of the doubt and say that you came over just to see me.

"I did Fiona, we're family."

"I said I was giving you the benefit of the doubt. Let's not go beyond that right now, okay?"

Connor huffed. "You know the reason that you're treating me like this is because that boy is back."

"Please Dad everything does not revolve around Lincoln."

Connor stood up and gave his daughter a stern look and shook his head.

"I can see this isn't a time for the both of us to talk."

"And when do you think would be a good time for us to talk, Dad?" Fiona hoped that her voice sounded sincere.

"Since you seem to be so busy, I'll make sure to give you a call, and we can arrange an appointment."

Fiona knew the worst part about dealing with her father was the guilt. He had a way of being able to make her feel so guilty even when she knew she was right.

"Fine, I'll be waiting for your call."

Connor stopped right before opening the door. He didn't turn around to face Fiona, instead he just spoke in a low tone.

"I'm sure you'll be waiting for a call, but it won't be mine. Even now, that Chase boy has got you wrapped around his finger." With those words he pulled the door open and let himself out.

Fiona looked at the door and then screamed. This was what it was always about the endless guilt she felt whenever she had to tell her father no. What made it worse was that even after living here for so many years with her father, she still didn't have a better way of handling it than when she was a teenager.

"I'm surprised you decided to come work in the office," Fiona said to Veronica. "I usually have to pull teeth to get you to come in."

Fiona watched as a Veronica squirmed in her seat. There was a rumor running around town. Well there was always a rumor running around their small town. But the talk that seemed to have gotten everyone's attention was that Lincoln showed up at the office in the mornings with his cat.

It seemed to Fiona, Veronica spent more time looking at the door then she did trying to write a grant. She could understand why everybody was so enamored with Lincoln. He had come a long way from that scrawny boy before. Fiona just couldn't leave it alone.

"Veronica, are you waiting for something?"

Veronica turned to look at Fiona and smiled. For a moment, Fiona thought the smile must have look like the one on shark gave a guppy right before he eats. Not willing to back down, she smiled back.

"Oh no, I'm not waiting for anything, I was just thinking that maybe it makes more sense to keep the door open, you know, so we can get a little air in here."

"I feel just fine, Veronica, maybe you should think

about working from home where you know you have central air and privacy to do your work."

"I can see I came in the nick of time. You do seem like you need some company around unless you are already expecting some?"

Fiona didn't even respond to the question. Two hours later, Veronica packed up her bag.

"Will I be seeing you tomorrow, Veronica?"

"No, no, I won't be in. I'm sure you'll be disappointed. I think I can get more work done at home, after all."

At first, Fiona was disappointed and thrilled that Lincoln hadn't shown up. Ten minutes after Veronica left, Lincoln walked in.

"Did you see Veronica?"

Lincoln shrugged. "It was hard not to see and hear her when she came into the office."

"When she came into the office? You mean you saw her when she came into the office?"

"Aster and I both saw her come in, and we waited patiently for her to leave."

Fiona could barely hold back her smile. "You do know she wants to have dinner with you and get to know you a little better?"

Lincoln shrugged.

"So is this the new Lincoln who ducks and dodges females hot on his trail?" she muttered.

"Normally, I don't avoid women like that. But she seems to be a little bit more aggressive than the average woman."

Fiona stopped and gave him a smirk. "Please don't tell me you're scared of Veronica…"

"I'm not scared of her. I'm cautious. Cautious people live to see the next day and tell the tale."

"Okay Mr. Cautious, you're here. What can I do for you?"

"I thought I would suggest a place where we could meet. It seems like me coming to see you at the office is becoming a town spectacle."

"Do you care what the child sees or doesn't see?"

Lincoln smiled. "That is a funny question for you to ask."

Fiona was about to answer back something sassy and smart, but when she thought about it, she did have a lot of gall to go ahead and say that to him. He was the guy she always met in a secret place and never in public. That wasn't because she was ashamed of Lincoln. It was one more thing that her father had asked her to do that she had done blindly.

"I'm sorry, you're right. So where did you want this meet up today?"

He moved in a little closer to her. "I'm thinking we should start at the beginning."

"Have you even been there lately? I don't even know if the spot has grown over or been taken over by some animals."

"I have been there and it's been all prepared."

"Prepared?" If it was prepared, that meant he had a plan. The thought that he was planning sent a tingle up her spine.

He walked out the door, leaving Fiona to her thoughts. What exactly did he mean by prepared? This Lincoln was definitely not the boy from the days gone past. It took everything in her not to look at him as he walked away. There was an exhilaration that came with the unknown. There was an element of surprise that came with Lincoln.

She couldn't wait to discover this new Lincoln.

Thirteen

Connor turned the doorknob and it was locked.

"Missed her!" Connor said jokingly standing in front of the door.

Fiona could have had an office anywhere in town. He never understood why she wanted to have the office at one of the two ends. Oh Connor knew about her daily walks but he always thought she should have an office that was somewhere in the middle of town. He wanted everyone to see his daughter and know how important she was. He walked down the ramp and decided maybe he'd go get some coffee.

Connor didn't have a lot of close friends. It wasn't because he didn't want them, it was just that he was different. He knew he was different when he was a young boy. Numbers came easy to him. His childhood had been spent with people asking him to do tricks. Kids would ask him to add four and five numbers at a time. He hoped if he did, they would be his friends. At the end of the day, when the tricks were over, they all left him.

He didn't like to do the things the other boys liked to do either. He didn't mind fishing, but he'd rather be reading a book, adding numbers, or building something with his hands. It wasn't until he was in elementary school that he realized he had a problem reading. Elementary school and high school can be cruel. He had no real friends; there was no one to stick up for him when the bullies came. He always wanted to leave Rolling Springs. He just wasn't smart enough. Connor knew that if he ever had a child, he'd make sure that child didn't get stuck in Rolling Springs too.

When he had met Fiona's mother it was the best day of his life. She was an outsider with a job at the hotel in town. She thought his peculiarities about working with numbers was a gift. It was enough of a gift to get her to marry him. As time went on, she discovered that the people of rolling Springs did not agree with her about his gift. No one wanted to visit her because they were scared that whatever it was that Connor had might get on their children too. When Fiona was born and she showed some of those same gifts, it was too much for Fiona's mother.

One night he heard Fiona's mother crying, and in the morning she was gone. Just as Connor was settling into his painful memories he heard his name being called.

"Hey, Connor!"

Connor turned to see who it was. It was his friend Ian hobbling along trying to catch up to him.

"You didn't hear me, I've been calling you for at least half a block."

Connor shook hands with Cal as he made it to him.

"Cal, you know you shouldn't be running. What happens if your heart starts acting up again?"

Cal waved Hunter's comments away.

"You know my thoughts, Connor. When it's your time, it's your time. Where are you off to anyway?" Cal laughed.

"Going to get coffee from the shop."

"Well since you're going anyway, I don't mind going if you're buying," said Cal.

"Sure, let's go."

Once they were seated at their table outside of the coffee shop, Connor leaned back and smiled, looking up into the sky.

"So did you go see Fiona this morning?"

Connor didn't want to talk about Fiona.

"You can try and avoid this question all you want. I want you to know that I am a professional waiter. I did a lot of waiting in my marriage before my wife died, and I'm pretty sure I can wait for your answers too."

"I did go to see her, but she wasn't in. I'm trying to do the right thing."

"I can tell that you were not happy that the Chase boy's back."

"I know, I know, you think I should just let her do whatever she wants. You think that I've interfered more than my fair share in their lives earlier."

"Connor, I'm saying kids will be kids," Cal said. "I may not know all of the ins and out about what happened between you and Fiona and the Chase boy, but what I will tell you is whatever it is, let it go. Girls are little different than boys. I lost touch with my daughter and almost lost the opportunity to see my grandkids."

"She wasted herself because of that boy."

"She's the town treasurer," Cal countered.

"It's not enough! She's somewhere on the end of town and people come by and ask her to do numbers. She should have been more. She should have been able to leave Rolling Springs. Chase left, and he had the same problem she did. I only wanted the best for Fiona."

Cal gave him a long look.

"I think you need to look at Fiona again. This time when you look at her, make sure you see her, and you don't see yourself, Connor. Children are a wonderful thing. They come into your life and give it purpose, regardless if you are ready or not. Sometimes, though, one of them will come into your life and they will show you everything that you thought was right was really wrong."

"And you know this how? You have your kids. None of them live here in Rolling Springs."

Connor put a couple of dollars on the table and then rose.

"I don't need your words of wisdom Cal. I need to make sure I do right by my daughter."

Cal reached out and tapped the table.

Connor looked back to see what the noise was.

"I'm your friend Connor. When you get out of your way, give me a call and we can sit down and talk about what to do about Fiona."

Connor turned and kept walking. He wasn't sure where he was going. He just needed to walk. Cal just didn't understand. He knew what he was talking about. Connor knew he was the one who was really responsible. At the end of the day Connor knew it was all his fault that Fiona was still in Rolling Springs and he promised himself every day he'd try to do right by her and set her free from this place.

"Are you in here, Fiona?"

Fiona turned and saw Lincoln walking into her office. Does he wake up looking edible? she thought. He was in front of her desk in three strides. Three strides for her to see a body moving in perfection. She used to think she liked bulkier men, but Lincoln was proving her wrong. He was long in the legs and muscular in the torso. Not so much muscle he'd burst a shirt but definitely enough so his muscles would play peek a boo with the sleeves of a shirt. Then it was topped off by a face that could have been a professor's, if it wasn't for the intensity of his gaze and the lack of glasses.

He might have had a scholarly look but Fiona had to admit that once she looked at his lips, everything academic left her thoughts and the only thing she could think of was, when would he kiss her again?

"Hi, do you have time for me?"

"I might be able to put aside some of these numbers since you're an old friend and all."

Fiona had to shake herself mentally. What was she doing having this easy banter with Lincoln? Feminine curiosity warred with logical caution. Was she supposed to stand up? Was she supposed to run up and hug him now? What were the rules when you were trying to get back together with your first love? She couldn't do this.

"Fiona, stop," Lincoln said. "You are making this more complicated than it needs to be."

"I'm doing what?"

"You are worried about us and how this works?"

"Why would you say that?"

"Because that has always been your way. If you don't know how everything is supposed to happen, you get crabby."

"You seem to like to throw that word around a lot around me. Maybe I'm too crabby to be in a relationship."

"No, I think you have just enough crabbiness to deal with me," he said with a grin.

"You are not helping."

Holding up his hands he waved at her. "Fiona, I have an idea. We should discuss what my plan is. Can you meet in our spot tomorrow?"

"Of course."

"Great, we'll talk there and go over what needs to be done. By the way, I wanted you to know all is going well with the center. So I'll see you early morning. Just like old times?"

She nodded.

"Tomorrow then."

How did he do that? Every time the man came in, he said something that changed her world, and then he left, leaving her feeling excited, invigorated and scared all at the same time. Maybe tomorrow she'd be able to—

Then it really hit her. She was going to go meet Lincoln Chase, the man with more money than king Midas, to rekindle their love. Lincoln had been around the globe twice. He'd been seen with some of the most beautiful women in the world on his arm and she was going to try to rekindle something.

He probably didn't realize it, but he was used to

women who primped and prepared. The last time Fiona primped was when she put a masque in her hair. She only did that because she had leftover cucumbers. Fiona leaned back in her chair and let her head loll back. There was no way she would fit his mold. She'd meet him tomorrow, but she'd have to tell him then she wasn't the one for him and that she couldn't be beautiful, well-coordinated and magazine-worthy like the other women she had seen on his arm.

Fourteen

Lincoln sat on the bench underneath the white gazebo. He waited patiently for Fiona to show up. He had gotten some work done on their site for the last couple of days. Now, in order to get to the site, there was a well-defined path, lined with small white boulders on both sides, that led to the clearing where two tree stumps still stood. Instead of the tree stumps being used as seats, they were covered and transformed into small makeshift tables.

He had his personal chef make up some cinnamon confections. They were arranged on the table atop the most elegant plastic table cloth in Rolling Springs. Next to the Confections were two carafes of coffee. One was hazelnut and the other one was French vanilla. They say the way to a man's heart is his stomach. He was more than willing to see if it worked with Fiona as well.

He was looking at the arrangement and thinking about redoing the whole thing when he saw Aster come down the path. She had a white linen and satin lace bow tied around her neck. Her coming down the pathway meant that Fiona was on her way. Or, at the very least, somebody was on their way.

Fiona came around the corner, and she looked a little hesitant. She walked down the path dressed in a white sundress. Her hair was loose and flowing about her shoulders, and Fiona had on the cutest sandals ever. He couldn't recall a time when she had been so beautiful. As usual, she wore no makeup but her skin glowed bright as a pearl.

She might have dressed for this occasion, but there were little nuances that said she was still his Fiona. Practicality was always on her mind. On her wrist were hair bands to pull her hair back into a ponytail when her hair started to aggravate her.

It wouldn't have mattered to him what she wore. He would have still been able to see his Fiona. She was the woman who had graceful moves and a peaceful aura.

"I thought I was going to beat you here," she said.

"I couldn't let that happen. Besides I had to make sure that it was prepared for you," he said as he gestured to the table.

She smiled. "All of this looks so impressive. I'm not even sure when you had the time to do it.

"I wanted to make sure we started off right, so I decided to make an impression."

"Pat yourself on the back. Your mission was accomplished. But all of this," she said as she gestured around her, "Is exactly the reason why I don't think this is going to work."

"You don't like my taste in designs?"

She shifted her way to her right foot and then crossed her arms in front of her chest. Maybe this was too much for her? Maybe he was pushing her too fast?

"It's not going to work between us," she stated in a no-nonsense tone.

"You don't even know if the pastries are bad or not. It's true I could have probably chosen another color besides white, but white was the easiest thing with the time—"

She waved her hands in the air to stop him from talking.

"No, I'm not talking about the design or the food. What I'm talking about is this thing between us. I don't think I can do this with you."

Lincoln had the breath knocked out of him. He slumped a little bit and Aster jumped into his lap as if she knew he needed someone to comfort him.

"Do you want to tell me what's wrong with me?"

"It's not what's wrong with you. It's the world you live in and where you are in life right now."

Lincoln turn the words over in his mind, trying to understand precisely what Fiona was saying.

"Is it because I live in the city, or is it because I run a company?"

"No, you!" She pointed at the table. "This whole setup."

Lincoln looked around and tried to understand. He had ordered a white gazebo to be built in the spot where they used to meet, so she wouldn't have to worry about falling leaves. When they were younger she used to always jump whenever she thought something had fallen in her hair. The dessert on the table was one of her favorite foods, and he even had coffee. To make sure she was comfortable, the seats had cushions. Lincoln checked his own clothing. Today he had decided to dress casually. He had on a dark blue button-up shirt, and blue jeans. Aster was on his lap, but that's where she was most of the time. His hair was in place, and he had taken a shower. He just didn't know what exactly it was she was referring to.

Lincoln knew there was something different about him. He had always been the odd man out. If whatever that thing was, was so big that even Fiona couldn't be with him, then there wasn't any hope at all.

"I don't want to beat a dead horse, but can you tell me what is it exactly that you find offensive about me?"

Her eyes widened and she gave a nervous laugh. "Offensive? I never said that there was something about you that was offensive. What I'm trying to say is this is all over the top. You do everything to perfection. You set up this place, and it looks beautiful and perfect. You even have a cat that is beautiful, perfect, and exotic." She looked down at herself and then spoke in a tone so low he could barely hear her. "I'm not any of those things, Lincoln."

Lincoln wanted to jump up for joy. He completely understood what it meant to be insecure about who you were around other people.

"Fiona, you know me. There are a lot of words people use to describe me, but perfect isn't one of them."

She looked from side to side as if the answer was going to come to her from somewhere. "Listen, I'm not perfect. I'm not extraordinarily beautiful like the women I used to see on your arm in the newspapers. Most of all, I don't have gobs and gobs of money in order to meet the expectation that I think you take for granted in your life."

"So you want me to give up my money and get a bad haircut?"

"What?"

"What I'm saying to you, Fiona, is I'm willing to do whatever it is that you want. Those women that you saw on my shoulder weren't with me for me. They were with me because they were hoping that they would be able to get a step up. I don't think most of them even knew I was a person."

"Lincoln, you are amazing!"

"You see me that way, Fiona. That's why I had this gazebo built and I had this whole area redone. No one sees me the way that you see me."

She let out a big sigh.

"You already know I'm crabby."

"I thought we went over that already, and that's not a problem."

He put Aster down and then went to stand in front of her.

"I want you to know this isn't easy for me either. When I look at you, I see the best of everything I could have had. I'm scared you'll find that you don't like the man as much as you liked the boy." He looked at her and smiled. Then he reached out and touched her hair behind her ear.

"You think you're stepping into the unknown because I have money. I'm stepping into unknown territory as well. When it comes to feelings, no one's going to say I know how to do that well."

"Lincoln, when you set your mind to something, you get it. I've always admired that about you."

"It's not about setting my mind to something. It's about having the courage to grab onto something that you're not sure you can actually keep. I'm scared, but you are so worth it. I need to know if you feel the same way."

She reached up and placed her hand on his cheek.

"I do feel the same way. And just for the record, you don't have to change who you are. So far, I love the man just as much as I love the boy."

Just then, Aster walked between them, slightly nudging their feet.

Fiona stepped back.

"Well, I guess that's a sign it's time for us to eat."

He smiled back at her. "I hope these things taste as good cold as they do warm."

"There's only one way to find out."

They both went to the table and took a seat. Fiona opened the basket and took two cinnamon rolls out for each of them. Lincoln poured coffee for them, and they sat down and looked across the table at one another.

"Bon appetit," Fiona said as she took the first bite of the pastry.

Her eyes popped open, and then her eyelids slowly descended. She gave a low moan of pleasure and then her tongue came out and licked the icing off of her lips.

Lincoln stared at her. His cinnamon was halfway to his mouth. This was Fiona. He didn't understand why she was worried about those other women. If only she could see herself the way he saw her now, she'd know no other woman could compare to her on any front. The most important thing was that he always knew what she was feeling. Fiona never bothered to hide anything. When she was happy, she was happy. And obviously when she enjoyed eating her cinnamon rolls she went all in.

"So-o, I think this is a good time for us to talk about when we will be meeting here."

"Can you wait until I'm done with this cinnamon

roll? I mean this is so good nothing should interfere with the experience."

"And you don't think what I'm talking about is going to be pleasurable to us both?"

"Wow that's a tall order. Besides we should probably do one thing at a time so we can savor the moment."

He put his cinnamon roll down and waited. He watched her a couple of more times and then her eyes opened.

"Okay, okay I can't possibly eat this knowing you're looking at me."

He reached out and took a sip of his coffee.

"I think you should get used to me looking at you a lot. It's going to be pretty hard not to look at you while we're having a relationship."

"You can look at me. I just don't want you ogling me all day with puppy dog eyes."

"You don't think it's romantic that I'm obsessed with you and I need to look at you all the time?"

"No," she said with a shudder.

"That's good. I think that's kind of creepy too. I have to ask about these things. I once dated a woman who wanted me to look at her all the time otherwise she thought I was looking at other women."

"Really?"

"Really. So let's set some ground rules."

"I love those."

"The first rule is we'll always meet here."

"What happens if it rains?"

"The gazebo has a shell that goes over the top if it rains, or if it's windy, we can actually pull down the external walls and will be fine."

"You have thought of everything."

"This gazebo was long in the making."

"Okay what else?" Fiona asked, fascinated that Lincoln had put so much planning and forethought into it. She knew he was a planner, but that he'd plan all this for her was exhilarating.

Lincoln put his coffee cup down and then sat back as far as he could without falling off the bench. As if on cue, Aster jumped onto his lap.

"You know it's not all about what I want to do Fiona. If you want to make a rule as well, let me know. I think we should both contribute to this."

Fiona smiled. "Thank you for offering, but I'm going to let you lead for now."

Lincoln reached over to the side of the bench and pulled up a white box and placed it on the table. He pushed the box toward Fiona.

"What's this?"

"Open it."

He watched her pull the box toward her and then give him a wary look. She opened the white box, and inside was a necklace with a delicate silver chain. When she held it up, there was a charm on it. The charm was a little house.

"I remembered you're allergic to gold."

"Yes, you did," she replied in a shaky voice.

"When we were younger, you said that new beginnings always start at home. This is our new beginning, so I thought the charm would be appropriate."

Fiona sniffed.

"I didn't want to make you cry, Fiona."

"I know. It's just- just. Don't mind me. Thank you, Lincoln."

"May I put it on you?"

She looked up at him as if she were thinking about running away. Then in the last moment, he saw her throw her shoulders back and nod yes. He reached for the necklace and the both of them stood up to come around the table. Lincoln ignored Aster's meow of disapproval at being moved before she was ready.

He stood with the necklace open waiting for Fiona.

"You have it backwards, Lincoln."

"No I don't. The charm is facing me, that means you are going to have to get close enough to me that I can put it around your neck. Do you think you can do that?"

She nodded and took two more steps closer to him.

"I promise I'm not the boogey man, and I can confirm I've bathed today."

She laughed and took another step toward him so that his hands were around her neck. He looked her in the eye and fastened the necklace on her. This was his Fiona. She was strong, bold and faced her fears head on.

"This is where it begins for us, Fiona," he said softly.

Lincoln wasn't sure if it was his heartbeat or hers that was so loud. There was a rush of blood going through his body, and he had to fight the urge to rest his hands on her shoulders and pull her into his embrace.

"I think this is a good first step."

"You're right, we should go."

"I agree. The only thing missing is my goodbye kiss," he said with a grin.

"You still want that?" she said in a trembling voice.

Lincoln had hoped she would want that.

"I can wait if you're not ready. We've got time."

Just as he was stepping away, she grabbed him by his shoulders.

"We do have time and we shouldn't waste it on fear."

She pulled his head down, closed her eyes and kissed him. He could feel her hand tensing on his neck and her body begin to sway in his arms. Then she drew back.

The both of them were breathing a little harder. Just when he thought she would kiss him again a car drove by and broke the mood. They both laughed nervously.

"So I'll see you here in two days?"

"Two days?" she asked.

"I still have to make sure Irma and Dione don't bankrupt me with new demands," he said.

"Fine, in two days."

"Now about those pastries." They both turned to the table and sitting on the table licking her paws was Aster.

"It looks like we don't have to worry about those pastries after all," Lincoln said, and they both began to laugh.

Fifteen

"It's a full body suit and a shirt to cover you," Lincoln said, handing her the bathing suit and the wrap to go over it.

Fiona eyes the clothing suspiciously. "You just want me to be naked?"

"It's true one day I hope to have the privilege of seeing you as a husband does a wife, but today I wanted to get rid of this issue of perfection. This will put us on equal ground.

Two days later, she was back, and Lincoln was once again already there when she arrived. She found the last two days she had been a ball of nerves in anticipation of this day. She really needed to get a grip. After all, this was Lincoln, and maybe if she kept repeating that mantra to herself she'd be able to calm the nerves that were running amok in her. The truth of the matter was their last meeting still sent tingles down her spine when she thought about it. If that's what he did as an intro, what was going to happen as they got closer to one another?

They stood facing each other in front of the table. She knew and trusted Lincoln. Still, the idea he'd suggested made her feel shy in all sorts of weird ways. It wasn't like she had never worn a bathing suit, so that wasn't the problem. If she were honest, the real problem was he was going to see her arms and legs. She was sure she had wings. She didn't have large hanging flaps of flesh from her arms, enough fly away on, but there were still little chicken wings. Still enough to make a person say, maybe you shouldn't get into a bathing suit. He stood there smiling, and she took a deep breath. She wasn't going to let fear get in the way. He said this was about dispelling the whole beauty problem. Well better to get it over with quickly and let him be disappointed early. Fiona believed in ripping the Band-Aid off and this would be no different.

Pasting a smile on her face, she took the bag and then went into the side woods to change.

"Fiona where are you going?"

"To change. I know you don't expect me to change in front of you!"

Lincoln laughed. "Look over there behind the tree. There's a small temporary shelter I had them put together so you could change over there."

She looked at him and was once again taken back of how considerate he was. She went to the shelter and put on the bathing suit. It was a full-cut outfit, and it covered her, so she couldn't complain. Now she just had to leave the shelter and face him.

She wanted to stay inside and call out that she had changed her mind. Taking a deep breath, she opened the door and walked out. She was about to make excuses for her body when she saw him.

She stared at him, but more importantly she stared at the "Y" incision on his chest.

"What happened?" she asked, pointing to his chest. "I-I didn't know."

His eyebrow rose. "Is there a problem?"

"No, no your fine. I-I just didn't know."

"Didn't know about?"

She knew her eyes were wide open and she waited.

"You're not going to go explain that?"

Then he pointed to his chest. "Oh you mean this?"

"Well, yes"

He smiled. "I had a heart issue, and they needed to crack me open. I'm fine now. Is the scar offensive to you?"

"No, what kind of person do you think I am?" she asked him.

He laughed and held out his hand. "Come on, I wanted us to take a swim, and when we come out, lunch will be here."

She took his hand and then he led the way to the lake. The water was a bit chilly but the heat radiating from him spread through her hand and flooded her body. When they had walked into the middle of the water, Lincoln pushed away into the middle of the lake and swam away. She watched him take long strokes. The water came up to her waist, and she had a chance to really look at the lake. He looked so comfortable out there. When he looked over his shoulder, he waved.

"Are you coming out? It's not deep. You can stand in it."

She shook her head. "I would love to, but I can't swim. So I'm good."

He looked shocked and then came toward her twice as fast as he went out there.

"Fiona, I'm so so sorry. I didn't know."

She held up her hands to stop him.

"Lincoln, please, it's okay."

He didn't stop. Instead of listening he grabbed her hand and guided her toward the bench. On the bench was two fluffy towels. He picked up a towel and held it out for her to walk into.

"Okay that was the quickest dip ever," she laughed.

When she walked into his arms he began to rub her like she was a lamp.

"I'm so sorry! I just wanted you to let you know that I was ugly too and— Not that I think you're ugly, but I wanted to make sure we were past this point and didn't look at our bodies like that.

Fiona pulled her arms out of the towel and grabbed his shoulders.

"Lincoln, I'm fine, and I'm not offended, and yes I'm glad we're both ugly," she said with a grin.

He stopped and sat the both of them down on the benches. Aster wound herself around his legs. He looked so defeated and lost, she reached over and tapped him on the shoulder.

"Well, I will say, this does bring back old times. I never knew what was going to happen when we would meet."

They both laughed.

"I have brunch for us," he said as he pointed to the basket. She watched him set up the table, and all she could think about was the scar on his chest. She tried not to look at it, but when he bent over and spread the food out, it almost looked like he was aggravating it.

"Does it bother you much?" he asked.

She reached out and placed her hand over his.

"It's not the scar, Lincoln. It's knowing I could have lost you. I could have lost us before we ever got started."

He smiled and nodded. The rest of the morning they talked about old times. They caught up on the people they knew and then laughed at how the Irma and Dione were still here and still together running the town.

After eating they both got dressed, and she started to collect the towels and place them on the table.

"What are you doing, Fiona?"

"I didn't want to leave a mess and—"

He walked over to her, took the towels from her hand and then helped her to her feet.

"I appreciate it, but I've got someone to do that for us." He reached out and touched the necklace with the charm on it. "You're wearing it."

She looked down at it and then at him.

"Well Lincoln, how is anyone going to know I'm taken if I don't wear this necklace? It's not a ring or anything, but it fits me."

"Thank you for coming out here today."

She placed her finger on his lips and shook her head. "There's no need to thank me. We're building this together, right?"

"Right," he said in a shaky voice. He kissed her on the cheek and then stepped back and offered his arm. "May I escort you to the car?"

She looked at his arm and was charmed and disappointed. This was the best date she'd been on in a while, and until this moment, she had thought it would end with a kiss like the last time. She plastered on a smile, and she put her arm in his. They walked to her car, and when she was sitting in the front seat with the engine running, she looked at him.

"It was definitely memorable," she said with a nervous laugh.

"It was. The only thing that would have made it perfect would have been a kiss, but I want you to know you control the time and what happens. So, thank you for an amazing time. And I'll text you our next meetup, okay?"

"Okay." She watched him go back to the site, and then she let her head rest on the steering wheel. She wanted to call out to him. Why hadn't she said something? Oh yes, this was definitely a memorable day. She cleared her mind and then drove off. It was a change to stop worrying about beauty and instead wonder when their next kiss would be.

Sixteen

Connor knocked on the office door. He had heard about the activities in the woods. Fiona was smart, but sometimes she just had a blind spot. It looked like that blind spot was Lincoln Chase.

He stepped in and waited for her to pick her head up from the books she was working on. When she gave him a curious look, he turned around and locked the door behind him.

"I suppose asking if this can wait isn't an option," she said tersely. "I was trying to finish up the numbers for the school and the yearly budget."

"I can't seem to find you at any place. You're always so busy now that I have to catch you when I can."

"You could always come by my place," she said defensively.

He shook his head. "I'm in town most of the time."

"You mean you won't come to the house because it's not your place."

Fiona's mouth was set in a firm line of disapproval and annoyance. Instead of continuing the issue that had been an unspoken elephant between them, she gestured for him to take a seat at the table.

"Coffee?" Fiona asked.

"No I've had my morning cup. I have to be careful with my health these days."

Fiona nodded and then sat back in her chair and waited.

"I wanted to talk to you," he said. "I feel like we haven't been able to really talk lately. Every time we are in the same room with each other, it just seems to go wrong, and it wasn't always like that."

He watched Fiona smooth her hands over her thighs and take a deep breath. Her hair was pulled up into one of those fancy knots that made her look all professional. She had on a cream-colored blouse with a rounded neckline, and around her neck hung a silver necklace with a home charm on it.

"Are you here to discuss why we don't talk? If you are, it's a little late. We haven't been talking freely for a long time, and you know why."

He held up his hands. "No, no, I'm not here to bring up the past." This wasn't the way he'd expected the conversation to go. He was hoping he could remind her of the time when they'd been close so he could convince her to rekindle that closeness. Now he found himself facing a woman who didn't long for the relationship they'd had when she was a child. That was a blow he wasn't really prepared for.

Fiona let out a breath and then crossed her arms over her chest.

She was his little girl, but she was so much more. While she wasn't aching for the lost time, he was. Certain aspects of her reminded him of her mother. He had loved Sophia so much, and when their marriage had fallen apart, he had done his best. It was hard to carry on when an image of the woman who hurt you woke you every morning and gave you hugs and kisses as if you were invincible.

Today she looked more like Sophia than he wanted to admit. She had that look of disapproval and that air of frustration. It was the look he'd gotten when she couldn't travel into town without being reminded that she was married to the human calculator. Sophia had wanted to fit into town so badly. She craved a social life and friends. Being with him had guaranteed that wouldn't happen. When she was done, she packed her bags and never looked back. Fiona knew her mom had left but she hadn't known her mom had sent him money with the divorce papers asking him to take the money and sign the divorce. She told him in a note she just wanted her freedom.

"Dad? Are you okay?" Fiona asked.

He put on a fake smile and looked at her. "Oh yes, I'm good. I was thinking about things."

"You mean you were thinking about Mom."

He didn't see any point in denying it. In fact, if he was going to save her, he knew he was going to have to put himself on the line. "I was."

"And?"

"And I always wondered why you stayed in this town after," he said. He'd thought after he had told her his inexcusable lie she would have moved away. He wasn't proud of his actions, but he'd done it to give Fiona had a better life. He could live with her hating him.

"Why would I leave? Everything I know is here,"

Fiona said. "I mean, I've gone away for a week or so and stayed in Airbnbs to see if I liked the town and the feel of things. You don't know this, but I've taken consulting jobs in other places. I wanted to know if I could make it in someplace besides Rolling Springs."

"You've consulted."

"Yes, Daddy. I've consulted," Fiona said with a slow smile.

"I always worried that you never saw anything else. And the times you consulted you never found another place you liked?"

Fiona shrugged. "I've seen beautiful places, Dad. I've seen caring and compassionate people, but at the end of the day, I wanted to come back home. This is where I wanted to be."

Connor looked at her and was confused. He understood what she was saying, but he didn't believe it. There had to something else for his daughter. Surely Rolling Springs wasn't going to be the end all for her.

"Dad, you closed the door and locked us both in here. What was it that you felt had to be done and with no interruption?"

Connor needed to find a way to make her understand. "Can I have some coffee after all?"

Fiona nodded. "Of course, I'll make you a cup. We got a Keurig in the office because it's my guilty pleasure," she said.

Ten minutes later, they were sitting at the table with coffee. He wasn't sure where to start, and he was happy to finally be able to sit with her in peace. There was a knock on the door and they looked toward it. The knock sounded once more and then nothing. They turned to one another and let out a nervous laugh.

Connor wasn't one for waiting, so after he had taken a couple of sips of his coffee, he decided to get to the heart of the matter.

"I hear you are seeing that Lincoln boy again."

He could see Fiona's body tense up at the very name.

"Daddy, I think we will have to agree to disagree when it comes to Lincoln."

Connor could see she was putting up her defenses.

"Don't do that to me, Fiona. Certainly a father has the right to ask his daughter about the man she is seeing?"

"You think you have right when it comes to Lincoln and me?"

"What I'm trying to say, Fiona, is that things are different now. It's not like the two of you are meeting in secret. I mean, look at you. You're actually wearing a necklace around your neck from that boy."

Fiona put her coffee cup down and pushed it away from herself.

"I think this meeting is done, Daddy."

Connor could see he had pushed too much too soon. But this was his daughter, and she was worth the fight.

"Fifi, I want you to think about this. Don't you think it's a little bit odd? He comes back to town and wants to start a relationship with you all over again. Now he's doing it in a public way. I'm scared that his motives aren't as clear as you may think."

"So what are you saying? That he's not telling me the truth? What other reason could he be here for?"

Connor peered to the side and then reached out across the table to grab her hand.

"I'm scared, Fifi, that he's here for revenge. Just think about it. The last time me and him met, I sent him away, and he left like a dog with his tail between his legs. Now he's back and wants to have a public relationship with you. No, I don't think he's there just for that. I think he's here to make a point to me. I think he's going to use you to get to me so he can get me back for what I did to him all those years ago."

Connor reached out across the table to Fiona and gently pulled her hands into his.

"It's your opinion that Lincoln isn't here for me. That he wasn't ever thinking about me. That it was only his urge to get revenge that made him come back to Rolling Springs. That revenge spurred him to help us out with a grant that he will be paying for. All of that for revenge, Daddy?"

Fiona got up and walked around. He thought she was finally seeing things his way. Then she walked right past him, unlocked the door and held it open. When she looked up at him, he could see her trembling smile and the glassiness of her eyes.

"I have things that I have to get done today. If you'll excuse me, please, why don't we pick this up some other time?"

He thought about trying to convince her to say something else, but there was such a look of hurt and defeat in her eyes that he just nodded and walked out the door.

"I would have never expected you to be here."

Lincoln gave Fiona a wan smile.

"It's my parents' old place. You must have a real issue to show up on my doorstep."

Fiona stood on the steps of Lincoln's place. Lincoln could see that Fiona was nervous, and he wanted to know what would bring her here without calling for them to meet at their spot. She was dressed in blue jeans and a pink tee shirt. Her hair was piled atop of her hair with the necklace about her neck. He didn't know what it was, but he'd fix it.

"We need to talk about something I need to clear between us."

"What is it? And do we have to talk about it on the front step?" Lincoln said, trying to make the moment a little lighter.

"It's not what but who."

She didn't even have to go any further. Lincoln knew this was about her father. He had tossed and turned about when this day would come. Would he be able to forget? Or at the very least, would he be able to forgive?

He stepped back to allow her to come in the door.

"We were going to have to address this eventually. Better that we do it now."

He walked her into his kitchen, and they sat at his table, which was elevated with chairs more like bar stools than kitchen seats. He looked in his refrigerator and pulled out some cinnamon desserts. He put them on the table and then pulled down two cups from the cupboard so he could make something to drink.

"Coffee, tea?"

"Coffee, please."

He made the coffee and brought it to the table before sitting down.

"I knew this day would come, and I think I'm ready, so please, help yourself to the sugar and talk away."

"Lincoln, oh, I need to talk about my dad, and I need to know that we are going to be able to get through this."

"We're not going to know unless you do it. So go for it."

"He makes me so crazy. He came to see me today and then he locked us both in my office. It just went downhill after that."

Lincoln listened to her rant as she picked up a Cinnabon and took a bite out of it. He waited for the old flood of anger to come. As he replayed each word Fiona said nothing happened.

"What went downhill after that? The rest of the day or the talk with your dad?"

"The talk. Keep up, okay? So he came in, and then he says he's worried about me. Worried that you're here because you want to get revenge and that you don't care about me at all. Oh, and before that, we started on the 'he never comes to my place' argument. And how we're not allowed to talk about my mother."

"I didn't know your father thought so much about me," he said sarcastically.

Fiona smirked at him.

"Aren't you the favorite one? We all noticed that you were more than just a genius."

"So you say, but it wasn't until later that the point was driven home."

"Oh yes, the first woman in your life."

Lincoln laughed at the comment. And sure enough, as if she knew they were talking about her, Aster came into the kitchen, eyeing the table like she was going to try to make the jump.

"I don't know what to do about him."

"I believe you."

Fiona took a bite out of the pastry and swallowed.

"You know even after everything he's done, I still feel guilty when we fight. The only thing that stops me from giving in to everything that he asks me for is that he always thinks it's about him."

Lincoln took another sip of his coffee and then put the cup down.

"Parents. You never quite know what to do with them. You can't treat them like business associates. You know that they're more than friends. The problem is, that while you're trying to figure out where they belong, they are busy trying to tell you where they belong. It can be overwhelming. In the beginning, they are supposed to lead. As you get old you and your parents are supposed to co-manage. When you get to be an adult, they should advise. When my mother isn't getting her way, she goes back to the role she had in the beginning where she gets to tell me what to do."

Fiona finished chewing the pastry and picked up another and pointed it at him as she spoke.

"You know, you're pretty smart about these things. Unfortunately, I'm still thinking I am the world's worst daughter. I mean, he always seems like he's trying to do the best thing, but in the worst way."

"What does that mean? Do you think I'm here just to get back at your father?"

"No, I know you're not. It's just in some ways, you have to admit, it would be easier if you were. Oh my goodness, I know I came here to talk to you about him, and I want to say thank you so much for listening. However, right now, I don't want to talk about him at all. Let's talk about us."

"I'm totally on board to talk about that subject."

Fiona laughed. "I bet you are on board with that subject. First things first, let's talk about the Learning Center. I've been doing the numbers and have to ask you again, are you sure that you want to gift back the grant money to the town? I know you have more than enough money, so that's not the issue. The real question here is there are a lot of new requirements coming up from Dione, and I just wanted to make sure that you were okay with it. If not, we can use the rent money."

"It is really challenging negotiating with a librarian and a principal. There are no books to handle these types of negotiation."

"Do you need help?"

"Are you saying you want to go in there with me?"

"No, no, no, I know better than to go into the room with those two women. But maybe what we can do is recruit some other older women."

"Ah, you want to do some consulting and outsourcing. I thought about it. I just don't think this is the way to go with It."

"If that's what your instinct says, then I think you should listen to it."

"You teased me by saying we were going to talk about us. Now that we talked about the Learning Center, let's talk about us. I'm going to open the floor up for you, Fiona. What questions do you have for me? You can ask anything."

He looked at her thinking deeply on the question. Finally, when she looked up at him with an expression of curiosity mixed with hesitation.

"I know you said you've always had problems with other people, but you're not hard on the eyes and you have gobs of money. How is it you never once got close to being married?"

He gazed directly into her eyes. "I'm going to answer this question, but I want you to remember that it's quid pro quo."

Her look became a little more wary as she understood his conditions.

"I will confess that there was a time I thought I was going to have to settle. It was right about the time I heard that you were engaged. There was a woman who I was meeting. We didn't care for each other, but we respected each other. Actually, when I look back on it, it was pretty sad. We both had given up on our true loves, and we just wanted to make sure that we didn't die alone."

"What happened?"

"She didn't like Aster."

She stared at him for a moment, like the words were sinking into her head, and then she burst out laughing.

"Okay, okay, that is enough of laughing at me. It's your turn. I know you are a rare find, Fiona. Why don't you have little Fionettes?"

"It's a funny thing. I've been engaged twice. Each time, they were men who were smart, and I think, men who were going places. That was probably the problem. I met them both when I was traveling away from Rolling Springs. I think that they couldn't imagine staying in Rolling Springs. The problem is I can't imagine staying anywhere else."

"Speaking about staying here in Rolling Springs. I forgot to give you something when we last met."

He stood up and held out his hand to her. She placed her hand in his, and he walked her into the living room.

He stopped in front of an end table on the side of his couch. On it was a white box. He turned, held it out and opened the box.

"Lincoln, really?"

"This is about us, Fiona, please take it."

She reached in the box and took the charm out. He placed the box on the side and watched her. Fiona took the heart shape charm and held it up.

"It's beautiful," she whispered.

"Please let me." He reached behind her and took off her necklace. He looped the heart onto it and then placed it back on her neck.

As he put it around her neck, she looked at the heart with her fingers angling it from side to side.

"Okay, I love the heart, but I want to know why you chose this?"

He was still behind her and trying to get the necklace looped again.

"I chose the heart because you need a home to start anew, but without love, it's empty. You have my heart and my love, Fiona."

He looked over her shoulder and watched her hands tremble against the charm.

"That is the sweetest thing ever, Lincoln. Have you closed the clasp? It didn't take you this long last time. Is everything okay?"

"I'm nervous, Fiona."

She stilled. "You're nervous?"

He gave a sharp laugh. "I get nervous, Fiona."

Finally, he had the necklace done.

"It's closed," he said.

They were stock still.

"Lincoln?" she whispered.

He moved closer to her and placed a kiss on her neck. Her heard the slight exclamation, and he stopped.

"Too much?"

"No, just unexpected. Again."

He placed his hands lightly on her hips and made sure she was okay with his move by waiting for her. "Are we okay?"

"Yes, Lincoln."

He drew in a breath and then moved closer to the other side of her neck. The only skin that touched was his lips to her neck. His body was still four inches from hers, but even at this distance, he could feel the heat radiating from her.

"Lincoln, I could turn around."

"I don't think that would be a good idea."

"Why not?"

Lincoln cleared his throat nervously. "Well I can tell you that from a business point of view everything is stacked in my favor right now. I have a beautiful woman that I love in my home. I also happen to have that seen beautiful woman in my arms. She and I are in my place, and I know she loves me. This could go a lot of ways, but it's not the way I want us to go. I want to make sure that whatever happens between us, is because we planned it, and not because the heat of the moment took over."

He leaned his forehead on her shoulder and took in two deep steadying breaths.

"I think we should meet up tomorrow."

"Is that your polite way of asking to me leave, Lincoln?"

"It's my polite way of saying we've only got one more charm to go, and I don't want to mess it up."

She stepped out of his arms and turned to give him a quick kiss on the cheek.

As Fiona went toward the door, she called out behind her. "I can't wait until we meet up tomorrow. Bye, Lincoln."

Lincoln heard the door close. He hadn't really trusted himself to just see her to the door. How often did a man get to hold the goal of his life in his arms and then had to let it go? He hoped that she had a good night's sleep tonight because he knew the only thing he was going to be thinking about when he went to bed was what could have happened and what didn't.

Seventeen

"You got that moonstruck 'I don't have any sense' kind of look on your face," Sherry said as she took a seat in the office.

"I invite you over to go get breakfast, and that's how you greet me?" asked Fiona.

"I guess I can greet you that way because I'm looking at your neck. And if I'm not mistaken, it seems as though you have two charms around your neck."

Fiona stopped and was pulled out of her euphoric reverie to really look at her best friend Sherry.

"What's the problem? Pease don't tell me that you're siding with my dad."

"Never!"

"I was getting scared there."

"As a general principle, I will never be siding with your father, but just for argument's sake what exactly is it that he saying?"

Fiona waved off the explanation.

"According to my father, Lincoln is here not because he wants to be with me but because he wants to get his final revenge on my father."

"Ouch! That was pretty rough. I stand by my original statement. No, I do not stand with your father on his thoughts. Although, you know what they say, a person thinks first that someone else is guilty of something that they would do."

"I hope that wasn't meant to make me feel better."

"From the way you were smiling when I came in this office, I'd say, you don't need help feeling better at all."

"I'm meeting him this afternoon. We're going out to lunch."

"Oh yes, this is a 'we're going to the same place we've gone to the last two times' kind of lunch?"

"We always meet at our spot. I think it's romantic."

"Well, as your best friend, I have to tell you, I can see how this man has all that money. He is definitely not spending it on romancing the women."

"Sherry, I need someone to be happy for me."

"I know," Sherry said with a sigh.

"That does not sound like the 'I know it's great and I have faith in this' kind of I know."

Sherry shrugged.

"I'm so happy that Lincoln came back to town. Just to see you smile the way I've seen you smile while he's here has been worth it. At the same time, this is going really fast, and I want you to be careful. Remember what your problems were before and make sure you all can stand against them now."

"I heard you. We are talking more this time. We even managed to talk about my father."

Sherry held her hands up defensively. "Remember, I'm not the enemy, Fiona. I just want to say, tread carefully."

"We're doing everything by the book."

"Make sure you're living in today and not yesterday, that's all I'm saying."

Fiona nodded." You're right. I just don't like it."

"Well, once again, your friend had come to the rescue and deliver sound and sage advice. We are ready to go to lunch."

"I thought we would just go to the coffee shop."

Sherry looked at her and raised her eyebrow.

"Oh yes, I can see his influence is already starting to rub off on you. But I want you to know, I will not be deterred. There is a brand new place that has opened up, and it looks pricey. We should go there."

"You're not even going to look at the reviews?"

"As small as Rolling Springs is, one of the high school kids probably wrote the review. We can't trust those. Now, let's go. Remember, you promised me food."

Fiona gathered her keys and then walked out the door behind Sherry. She needed to do something before her lunch date with Lincoln and this would be a good distraction.

She sat at the table with Lincoln. They had come to their site directly after work. She was so happy that she had worn her black pants and a white top. Lincoln had on a business casual outfit. He had on khakis and a light blue button-up shirt. By the time she arrived, he had already set the table.

"So what did you do? Have caterers up all night to finish this?" she said as she took a seat.

"No I didn't have a crew do this. In fact, I have been here for a couple of hours because I did it myself."

She looked around and saw he had white and gold balloons on the ground and hanging in the surrounding tree. The table was covered in a gold-colored table cloth with a white plastic one on top of it. The picnic basket had ribbons on it as well. She saw him place the paper plates in front of them both, and then he pulled out deli sandwiches and gave her half a sandwich as well.

"What's on the sandwiches?" she asked tentatively.

"They are all the same sandwich. Beef bologna and American cheese. I knew we both like to eat that because we ate it before."

"Good choice, then."

"I figured in the event you hated everything else, I didn't want it to end up like it did the last time, and you didn't get to eat something that you wanted." Lincoln laughed. "Your flexibility is one of the things that I really like about you."

"You're only saying that because it gives you the freedom to do replays," Fiona said.

"Well, I will admit, that I do like the fact you let me get away with doing replays. It's one of the things that money does afford me."

She finished the bite and swallowed. "If this is your idea of flirting with me, then I totally understand why dating hasn't gone so well for you."

"This is not me kicking my game, as they say. I'll have you know that since I have money most of the time there is no game to kick," said Lincoln.

"Wow, it's so nice to know that you haven't let that money go to your head."

Lincoln reached into the picnic basket. He pulled out

a bucket of coconut macarons. "I found these in a nearby bakery. I know you used to like these. Well, we both used to like the macarons a lot. It's not one of those French macarons with all those weird colors. It's the macarons where someone probably molded it with their hands, and it's popped it into the oven until it was toasty brown. I know that everyone is so concerned about their figure and BMI, but I was thinking that maybe just for today, we could do this."

Fiona nodded, and Lincoln cracked open the container. The coconut smell wafted in the air and brought back memories of days gone by. She remembered her and Lincoln laying on a blanket in this very area. The trees provided shade from the rising sun. Back then, when they were here, they would talk about their dreams and what they thought they were going to be when they got older.

She remembered the innocent way they laughed. When they were together, it seemed like nothing could stop them. She thought about how they laughed today, and she thought they had that same fearlessness.

Sliding back into old roles was easy. Lincoln was still the smartest man she had ever met. He wasn't arrogant. He wasn't prideful. Lincoln was silly and funny in his own way. When she was a child, she knew that she loved those attributes about him, but now that she was an adult, she appreciated those traits in ways that made her think about staying with him for more than just a day.

The first hint that something was coming was when a bunch of birds flew into the air. Fiona looked around, thinking that maybe it was Aster. When Lincoln looked over his shoulder as well, she knew it wasn't the cat.

"I knew I'd find you both here."

Fiona didn't want to even turn around. She'd know her father's voice anywhere. It was if the world was in slow motion. It was true, she had seen the birds flying in the air, but she hadn't heard a car. That meant that he had either driven up and parked far away and walked upon them, trying to spy on them, or even worse, somebody else drove him.

When she did look over her shoulder, indeed, there was her father.

"Hello, Dad."

Fiona looked at Lincoln, and for once, she wasn't sure. It was one thing to talk about her father, but this was the first time they were face to face. Lincoln stood up wiped his hands on a napkin and then went to her father and extended his hand.

"Mr. Dunn," he said waiting for her father to reciprocate the handshake. Grudgingly, her father shook his hand. Then he turned his attention to Fiona as if Lincoln wasn't even there.

"Why are you here, Fifi?"

Fiona put her hands on the table and let her head fall into them. Maybe if she ignored him, he'd go away.

"Daddy, we have tried to talk about this, and I think the best thing that we can do is wait. Wait until the both of us are in a better and calmer space."

"But I can't wait, Fifi. This is already going too far."

Then her father turned to face Lincoln. "You don't have children, Lincoln. So you can't understand that sometimes you have to do things for them that's the best for them even though they don't know it."

"Fiona isn't a child anymore."

"Fifi will always be my child."

Her father turned away from Lincoln as soon as he didn't get the response he was expecting.

"I know you think the ability that you have with numbers is a gift. I've got the same one, Fifi. And you know what? It doesn't always work out the right way. I wanted you to leave, to have something better than what I had."

Lincoln interjected. "So now you're trying to get Fiona to live out things you missed in your life?"

Her father swung his attention back to Lincoln. He pinned him with a gaze that would have normally made her shrivel up on the spot. However, Lincoln didn't seem to be moved.

"Who are you to interfere?"

"I'm Lincoln Chase. I'm the man he loves your daughter and always has."

"That's right, I know who you are, Lincoln Chase. Maybe but we need to go over what you're really doing here?"

Fiona wanted to get up and stop her father from saying all the awful things he'd said before.

Lincoln was faster. "I think my intentions are clear today like they were before. I just want to love and cherish your daughter."

"Is that why you've come back here, Lincoln?"

"She's the only reason I'd come back here."

Fiona watched them go at it. She had never been quick enough to respond to her father, and her feelings always got in the way. But the way that Lincoln was able to stand up to her dad made it seem like she was the most important thing in his life. She had known that Lincoln was kind and sweet. Now she knew something else. Lincoln could be fierce in defending the ones he cared about. Sherry had told her to be careful. Lincoln was showing her she didn't need to be."

Connor gave a mirthless laugh.

"Is she the first one, Lincoln? How many other women do you do this for? I bet you have a whole bunch of charms that you give to your women. We all know that you have lots of money. There's no need to go and come back to this little hick town for a woman. No need unless you had an ulterior motive."

Her father had disputed everything Lincoln had said. Then Fiona realized her father didn't think she was worth coming back for. She could feel the heat in her eyes, and she blinked back the tears that tried to fall."

"See, that's the problem. You don't truly know the treasure you have in Fiona. Fiona is more than a person who's really good with numbers. Although I have to say, I really do like that about her. She's funny, and she has an amazing sense of humor. She's also the bravest woman I know. She takes chances that others won't. And she finds the joy in things when everyone else is down."

Fiona wasn't sure if Lincoln really believed all of that, but the words were eloquent, beautiful, and moving. She wasn't sure if Lincoln actually saw her like that, but after hearing the words, she wanted him to have that opinion, but she knew she wasn't there yet. Her father had always taught her not to believe what others said, but only what you see.

"So, is that the way you're going to play it?"

"It's really not a game."

"The problem here, Lincoln, is that it won't be a game to her, but it will be just a bump in the road to you. I can see there's nothing I can say to make you feel different."

Fiona's father turned toward her and gave her a sad smile.

"When this is over, and he leaves you, I'll still be here."

Without saying another word, Fiona watched her father leave the clearing and walk away from them. She hadn't been involved in the discussion, but she still felt the urge to go to him and comfort him.

"She's wrong, but I still want to go to him," Fiona whispered.

"The fact that you want to go to him after everything that has happened just shows that you are a compassionate human being."

"Maybe. But there is something in me that just doesn't want to give up on my dad. I get that from him."

Lincoln turned back to Fiona and sat next to her on the bench.

"You do know what the true problem is, right?"

"I don't think I can take anymore today, Lincoln."

"He's lonely. There's nothing wrong with accepting that."

"But, there is, Lincoln. He's my father. He's the one who picked me up when I fell off bikes. He's the one who told me that everything would be okay, and I believed him. When he lied to me about the cancer, it was like my whole world had been shifted. What's even worse, is that there's still a part of me that wants that old relationship we had. The relationship where I could trust him. There's something in me that's also looking for a reason for why he does these things. And I may not like the answer, but if the answer is because he's lonely, then I'm part of the problem too."

Lincoln reached out and cupped her chin and lifted it, so they were gazing into one another's eyes.

"Listen to me. You can't be responsible for others for the rest of your life."

She looked at how earnest he was and knew he was speaking from experience.

"You're not a little girl anymore. He can't be the superhero he once was. He has to be the superhero he is today. I'm not telling you not to love him. I'm just saying make sure it's a healthy love where the both of you are getting something out of it, and he's not just pulling you."

"I'm sorry, Lincoln, I have to go."

"But—"

"This is all amazing right now. I think I need to be alone to think."

"Fiona, we can do this together. Don't run away and try to solve it on your own. We have each other now."

"I heard you, but I still just need some space, okay?"

She looked back at Lincoln, and his arms were hanging by his side, and he was looking into the ground in front of him. When she started to move, he didn't move. She had hoped he would say something, but when he didn't, she just got up and drove away.

Eighteen

It had been two days since she last saw Lincoln. Now Fiona stood on the steps of her father's house. It was this very moment, and this feeling that she dreaded. Undecided and unsure of what to do, she couldn't leave her father alone. When she had called him, and he asked her to come to his house, of course, she said yes. Fiona regretted that decision as soon as she had ended the call. During the last two days, Lincoln hadn't called. She didn't know if that meant that meeting her father was the last straw. She didn't know if that meant all the things he had said had just been for her father either. At any rate, it was too late to do anything about it. She was standing in front of her father's door, waiting for him to open it.

Her dad opened the door, and he greeted her with a smile. She could tell he had shaved, and he had on his Sunday best shirt.

"Come in, come in, Fifi," her father said, stepping aside for her to enter.

Hearing him call her that nickname was already putting her on edge. Today she had decided to wear a simple maxi dress. It was a rust color, and it had flowers around the hem. Her hair was in a ponytail, and she figured all around she was dressed in a way that wouldn't aggravate her father and would leave her comfortable.

"I'm so glad that you needed over."

"I'm always up for someone else to give me a free meal, dad." Fiona tried to lighten the situation, but her father just nodded and showed her to the table. When she took a seat at the table, she could tell that everything was brand new. She noticed the just-bought smell of things taken out of plastic. It gave her pause and made her look at her father a little differently. He was nervous too.

He came in with bowls of pasta and meat sauce. Then he sat down and urged Fiona to have some. It actually wasn't so bad. Fiona thought the food was good. But even more important, there wasn't a lot of talking going on. She was starting to think that maybe she could make it through this whole evening without them having to argue. When the evening was done, her father had put on some coffee and brought out dessert. Then he cleared his throat in an obvious way to get her attention. Fiona looked up and realized he was about to ask some questions. She was ashamed to say the first thing that came to her mind was relief that the night was over.

"Why did you stay in this town? I never thought it could give you enough, and I just never understood why you didn't take the first opportunity to get out."

Fiona smiled.

"Did you know that is the first time you've ever asked me that question? The answer to that question is, this is my home. I never wanted to leave for whatever it is that they called better."

"Didn't you wonder what else there was out there besides this little town?"

"I did. So I went out on weekends and took the consulting gigs here or there so I could see what it was like. I have to tell you, my feeling was, if I didn't like it in those short periods that I was there, then I probably wouldn't like living there."

Connor dropped his head to his hand and rubbed his forehead. Fiona could tell that her responses were not what he was expecting.

"I always thought that you wanted more. No, let me take that back. I always thought that if you saw other people were doing things and making a difference in other places, you'd want to be with them. You always want to help people, and I just thought this town was too small for you to grow to the person you could be."

"Is there something wrong with the person I am, Daddy?" she asked in a low whisper.

"No, Fifi. I want you to know this and believe this from me if you believe nothing else. You have never been a disappointment to me. Every day of my life, you have been the one thing that has made it worth me getting up in the morning. I guess because I feel so strongly about you, I wanted to make sure that you enjoyed life to the fullest."

Fiona could feel the heat behind your eyelids. She looked down into her coffee cup and blinked quickly.

"Thank you. I didn't know, and you never said it before, but thank you," Fiona swallowed and then cleared her own throat. "Since we are having this confession moment, I'd like to ask something."

"Please, go right ahead," her father said.

"Do not call me Fifi."

"I've always called you Fifi."

Fiona looked up to the heavens and closed her eyes.

"Yes, I am very aware that you have always called me Fifi. The problem is, I think Fifi sounds like the name of a small little poodle."

Her father gave her a confused look and then shook his head. "But when I say it—"

Fiona held up her hand to stop him before he finished.

"It's not about what your intentions are. It's about what it sounds like. It should also be about what makes me comfortable. I would appreciate it if you could call me Fiona."

"Okay, Fi—, I mean Fiona. That's going to take some doing."

"Thank you."

It was an odd thing, but right now, at this moment, Fiona felt relaxed. She wasn't waiting for the other shoe to drop. And she didn't feel as though her father was herding her or attacking her in a way to get her to do something he wanted. For the first time in a long time, she didn't have to watch every word she said.

"Thank you for coming over today. You know me, Fiona. I'm not one to say what's on my mind. You don't have to answer, but I have to ask. Are you really going to be with Lincoln Chase?"

Then it happened. Fiona had been lulled into some type of calm only to get ambushed by her father.

"It's no secret that Lincoln and I have been seeing each other," she said.

Connor held up his hands. "I can hear that tone in your voice, Fiona. I'm not going to say whatever it is I think is really going on. I just want you to allow me the opportunity to say something as your father. This man is from another world. You just finished telling me you never left because you love Rolling Springs. Lincoln left Rolling Springs, and it might be a nice place to visit, but like you, he may also want to go back to his life that his money can afford him."

"He did leave it, Dad, but he's from here. He understands what it means when I say that I love being home."

"I'm not saying that you all don't have something in common. What I'm saying is that it's very easy to look at the possibilities and sometimes overlook what's actually going to happen. He's a handsome man. He has a lot of money, and he seems to really enjoy being around you. I don't usually bring this up, but one of the reasons I'm concerned is because he reminds me of Sophia, uh, your mother.

I think that in the beginning, she loved Rolling Springs. It was close-knit, and it was everything she had dreamed about. The problem was, she was in love with certain parts of Rolling Springs. When I couldn't give her the other parts she thought came with it, or when she didn't see that she was going to get the dream she'd built in her head, she left. It took me a long time to get over that. I don't want to see you in that same place."

Fiona shrugged in helplessness, unsure of where this was going.

"So what are you trying to say to me, Dad? I'm not enough woman to keep him?"

Connor reached out across the table and covered her hand with his.

"I'm not saying any of those things, actually. What I'm saying is that Lincoln Chase was once from Rolling Springs. I think he's just outgrown living in Rolling

Springs. There may be some similarities between the boy you knew and the man that's here, but at the end of the day, that man has made his own world, and I just don't think Rolling Springs fits into it."

"Don't you think he thought about all of this? Don't you think our love will be enough?"

Connor pulled his hand back and grabbed his cup of coffee. She watched him look into the mug as if there was an answer in it. After a couple of moments of silence that were beginning to make Fiona uncomfortable, he looked up.

"I don't know how much you two love each other. I tend to think, that you two are like all couples. Right now, you think love conquers all. I thought that with Sophia. I can't tell you if love is enough or not. What I can say is, as your father, I don't want you to be hurt."

Fiona wanted to protest. However, if she put her heart on the side and thought with her head, she could actually understand what her father was saying.

"And you think I'm the one who gets hurt?"

Her father nodded. "Yes, Fiona. I do think it will be you. You put yourself into everything one hundred percent. If you love, you love everything you have. This man was from Rolling Springs, but the man he is now, travels in circles you've never seen."

Fiona wanted to say he was wrong. Again, when she thought about it with her head and not her heart, her father was right.

"Now, I could be wrong, Fiona. I just don't know if I'm willing to risk your heart on that, and when he gets up and goes back to his world, you will still be left here in Rolling Springs, having to deal with the consequences of this relationship not going right."

"I'm a big girl, Daddy. I think I can take some small-town gossip. I guess what I really wanted from you today was for you to be more supportive of me."

"I want the best for you, Fiona. My first duty, though, is to be your father. A lot of times that means I can't tell you what you want to hear, but I have to tell you the truth."

When he finished talking, there was a silence of finality in the air. Fiona couldn't really remember what else was said that night because her mind was in a fog. She knew she had changed the subject and small talk had happened. What kind of small talk? She couldn't recall.

It wasn't until she was in her bed that night that she really got a chance to digest everything that had been said. She had written out all the pros and cons of what her father had said, and each time, the only rebuttal she had on her side of the paper was, she was in love with Lincoln. Fiona had to remember she had been in love with Lincoln before, and he had left. He had left when he had nothing. Why did she think she could keep this man when he had everything? As she lay in her bed at night, her hands went to the necklace about her neck. Her fingers played with the house and the heart charms.

Then after tossing and turning for about two hours, she had made a decision. She unclasped the necklace and put it on her night table. She didn't have to like it, but her father was right. It was great to dream and live in la-la land for a little while, but at some point, you had to come home. Lincoln's home wasn't Rolling Springs anymore, but just like she needed to be home, she knew eventually Lincoln would need to go home too.

Nineteen

It had been several days since Lincoln had seen Fiona. When he woke up this morning, he decided it was time to face her and her father. He knew her father was never going to go away, and he had to accept that her father was going to be a part of Fiona and his life.

He wasn't sure he could talk about the past, but it was behind him now. He just wanted to get on with his life with Fiona, and if accepting her father was a part of that, then that was what he would do.

He waited for her to go for her morning walk. However, this morning, she hadn't shown up. After he walked Aster, he walked over to her office to see if she was okay.

Of course this morning, Aster needed more care than usual, so he didn't actually get there until an hour later. When he walked into the office, and she looked at him, he knew something was wrong.

There were no smiles and no light in her eyes that told him she was glad to see him. In fact, when he saw her, she looked wary. Maybe she was just upset because he had taken so long.

"Fiona, I didn't see you on your walk today. Are you okay?"

"I'm fine. I mean, I need to talk to you."

Lincoln could already feel the hairs on the back of his neck rising. Nothing ever good came from the words, 'I need to talk to you'.

"I've been thinking about what we've been doing, Lincoln, and I think it's just nostalgic."

"Nostalgic?"

"Yes, you know there's always a question about the one that got away. Always unanswered questions and possibilities about what we wanted to explore. What we could have done, but in the end, those possibilities don't matter as much because we've moved on."

"I want to thank you for helping us out with the grant and doing so much for the town, but I understand that this isn't your town anymore."

"Not my town," he echoed, confused.

"What I'm saying is that I don't think it's going to work out between the both of us."

Lincoln looked at her and was utterly confused. The only thing that brought him out of that reverie was when he saw a white box on the table. He picked it up and opened it. Inside was her necklace with the two charms.

"I just wanted to say, Lincoln, that—"

"Why did you give up on us, Fiona?"

She was speechless for a moment, and her mouth was moving, but no words came out.

"This is for the best, Lincoln."

"Best, according to who, Fiona?"

"You can't see this now but—"

"Tell me what happened, Fiona?"

"It's not a matter of happened. It's a matter of thinking things through."

"So all the rest of the time we were together you weren't thinking?"

"Don't twist my words, Lincoln. Don't make this any harder than it has to be. We just can't be. Our time came, and we missed it. I need you to accept that. Can you?"

"No. I see I made a mistake by leaving you too long. My heart can't accept this, but I will respect your wishes. I'll be in town for the next three days, and I'll finish up all the details with the grant. after that, I'll leave, and I won't bother you or remind you of missed opportunities."

He turned and walked out of her office. It wasn't what he wanted to do. He wanted to sit down there and talk things out, fight things out with her if need be so that she knew that what they had was so rare. But he couldn't fight it with emotions, so he decided to go back to what he knew. He'd make a plan. He'd get this right. He had three days. That was more than enough time to plan to take over.

If she just kept working, she wouldn't have to think about the pain. If she just kept working, she wouldn't have to think.

The front door to her office blew open as if a tornado had pushed it. However, standing in the doorway, was none other than her best friend, Sherry.

"Now, I know I told you to be careful, but I did not tell you to become a hermit."

"No, no, Sherry. I can't do this today."

"You can't do what exactly? You can't tell me why you decided to throw Lincoln away? You can't tell me what happened or what he did that made you think that he went from being the man of your dreams to being the man who will never be with you?"

"I don't know why you're so upset. You told me to be careful. I looked at everything, and I decided I just couldn't take that risk."

"You couldn't take that risk? You couldn't take that risk to have the love of a lifetime? This doesn't sound like you, Fiona."

Fiona let her head fall on to the desk, and she groaned.

"I'm tired. I wasn't sure what was going on when he was here, and now that Lincoln's gone, everything has changed. You know what the worst is, Sherry? It's the nights. When my mind is silent, and there's nothing to keep me occupied, I think of him. When I hear the birds chirping, and I turn and see that it's a cardinal. I think of him. He was the one who taught me what a cardinal sounded like. I can't even do my morning walks anymore because when I do, I think of him being across the street meeting me and coming over so we can both walk his cat. How sad is that I miss walking his cat with him?"

Sherry walked over and embraced Fiona.

"I know you're hurting. If you think this is what it has to be, then you know, I'll support you. I just want to make sure that you are making this decision and that the decision isn't coming from someone else's fears."

"Thank you," Fiona mumbled against her friend's shoulder.

"Well, you took all the sails out of my big speech I was going to make. Now that I look at you, you look more like a drowned rat, and because I'm your friend, I can't let you stay this way. So it's morning, where would you like to take me for breakfast?"

Fiona laughed. Sherry was the same. Right now, she needed something that was consistent and calming, and she'd take it wherever she could get it.

"Well then, my friend, let's go and find some breakfast."

Twenty

Lincoln couldn't believe he was standing here. What was so odd was this was the first time he had ever been here. He knocked on Connor Dunn's front door and waited for him to come to answer it. The door swung open, and Lincoln could see the moment of surprise cross over Connors face.

"What do you want?"

"It's not about what I want. This is about Fiona and what will make her happy," Lincoln said.

Lincoln thought Connor would hesitate, but instead, he came outside and closed the door behind him. That was fine with Lincoln; he didn't need to go into the house to have this conversation.

"Why are you here, Lincoln?"

"I'm here because we both love Fiona, and we both want what's best for her. But right now, we seem to be on the opposite sides."

"I don't know that we want the same thing for Fiona at all."

"You don't want her to be happy?"

"Of course, I do!"

"Then I'm going to need you to help me. We are going to have to get past our history to do right by the woman we both love."

"I haven't done anything," Connor protested.

Lincoln wanted to throw everything Connor had done back in his face. He wanted to tell him that Fiona had told him everything. Instead, he took a deep breath and tried to get his focus under control.

"We could both lose her now. Is whatever it is that you have against me worth taking that chance?"

Lincoln saw Connor take a step back and begin a mental retreat. Something had struck a chord with Connor. Lincoln wasn't sure what it was, but he wanted to press forward while he still had the advantage.

"I'm not looking to take her away from Rolling Springs, if that's what you are thinking."

"Really? How long do you think you can stay here?" Connor asked cautiously.

"Is that what you're really scared of? That I'm going to take Fiona away from you? You, above all people should know that she doesn't abandon those she loves. I need your help. If you don't give it, I'm still getting Fiona, but it will make her happy if we can at least tolerate being around each other."

"You've got all that money. I can't imagine what you need from me."

"What I need is for both of us to do this together. I have a plan. I want to know if you are willing to help me."

"Fiona already thinks the worst of me."

Lincoln smiled.

"Are her thoughts right?"

He saw Connor get very stiff. It even looked like he was about to say something to protest.

"I admit I can go too far," he said resolutely.

"Well, you know what they say. The first step is admitting you have a problem. I'm offering you an opportunity. I don't know if it's a second chance, but it would mean the world to her."

Connor looked like he was about to back out, so Lincoln asked him the final question.

"What do you have to lose?"

He saw Connor roll that thought over.

"I'll help you. What do you want to do?"

Fiona was having a craptastic day! The budget for the school had been rejected by the two-woman force for not having enough "wiggle room" in it. Fiona tried to call them back and explain that there was no quantity called wiggle room. They heard her speak, and then after talking for two hours, she agreed to go back to the drawing board and put in an additional fifteen thousand of wiggle room.

Then her dad called her and said he wanted to meet up. She was happy that they were talking, but she was still in such a down mood that she wasn't sure that she should go. She was going to refuse, but then he said it was important. And that was how she found herself sitting in the car with her father as they drove along. Fiona was so distracted she didn't notice until it was too late that they had driven right to her and Lincoln's spot.

Her and Lincoln. There wasn't a her and Lincoln. Today was the third day, and she was sure he was already gone.

"Dad I don't think I can—"

"Come on, Fiona. Let an old man make up where it started. I know this place has meaning for you. It has meaning to me too."

Fiona wasn't sure if she should laugh hysterically or cry. She blew out a breath and nodded. Her thought was maybe if I get all of the bad things out at once, then I'll have nowhere to go but up.

When they got out of the car, her dad was standing in front of it with a blindfold.

"Dad?"

Connor laughed. "I want to make things right, so indulge your old man and let me walk you to the surprise."

"A surprise? Really, we don't need to—"

"Hey, this is about an old man making it better. It might not be what you want, but it's what this old man could do."

Guilt upon guilt upon guilt.

"Okay, Dad," she said as she dug up a small smile.

He tied the blindfold around her and walked her along the path. She could've told him she didn't need him to walk her. She knew this path with her eyes closed. With each step in the dark, she saw visions of her and Lincoln. It was eighteen steps. How sad was that, that she knew?

"Okay, Fifi."

So much for the indulgence. Fiona reached up and pulled the blindfold away.

"Dad, I told you I don't—"

The words were caught in her throat. All around her dangled crystals of every color. The table was decorated with formal settings, and in the midst of it all was Lincoln in a dark suit and Aster with a bow tie.

Fiona turned to her father with tears in her eyes.

"Go on, Fifi. I know you don't like it, but old dogs can't change everything about them. Go to him."

She threw her arms around him and tried to speak through her choked throat.

"Thank you, Daddy."

When he let her go, he smiled at her, and she saw the tears forming in his eyes.

"Go on before I change my mind."

She went to Lincoln, and he dropped Aster's leash and embraced her.

"You're here."

"I had to wait. I knew you'd get the right answer eventually, but I wanted to give you time," he said.

"Getting my dad to bring me here was giving me time?"

"I'm working on my flaws. I hope you want to stay with me and help me out."

"Well, after careful consideration and looking at how much in need you are, I don't see how I could say no."

"Great! Then that makes the last part easy."

Fiona looked at him, confused. Then Lincoln brought out a white box.

"My charms and necklace! Thank you so much. I missed them so much." She opened the box, and her hands went to her mouth.

Inside there was a silver band ring with a heart-shaped diamond.

"Lincoln"

"This is the charm to replace them all. Fiona Dunn, will you marry me?"

She looked at him and then the ring when she heard Sherry call out, "Yes, she will!"

Fiona looked behind Lincoln and saw her best friend urging her on.

"Yes, Lincoln Chase. I will marry you."

He bent down and placed a kiss on her lips. Just as he was about to angle his head to deepen the kiss, they both heard her father.

"You two will have plenty of time to do that later. We have people waiting and a celebration to do."

They smiled at her father, and Lincoln looked into her eyes.

"I love you, Fiona."

"I love you too, Lincoln."

Both of them felt a feline body winding around their legs, and they looked down at Aster and said in unison.

"We love you too, Aster."

I hope you enjoyed Lincoln and Fiona's story. If you'd like to read another second chance romance Check out *Trust Us* for book six of the Love Endures series and read Pearla and Evan's story. If you've enjoyed reading this book, please take a moment to write a review.

Sign up to my newsletter to receive updates on new releases, sale promotions, and free books.

susanwarnerauthor.com

Enjoy a sneak peek of book 6

TRUST *Us*

One

"An attractive man has just asked me to marry him," Pearla Isaacs explained to her empty car. "He's stable, rich, and he's sending me to a class to interview the chef for our engagement party. Any other woman would be happy, why not me?"

As the owner of a project management company, anyone would think that having everything laid out for her would be a dream come true. Pearla had been working since seven that morning when she had received the evening invite from Lance Gorman, the bachelor millionaire who owned one of the most extensive support staffing networks in New York. He had called her and asked her to marry him.

The request took Pearla by surprise, and she wasn't able to respond right away. Lance filled in the silence with the good reasons they should marry. They had complementary businesses. He'd counted their business meetings as sufficient 'dates'. They had their own money and wouldn't be offended by a prenup, but the most essential factor was they were both past that stage in their life when they believed in love. He didn't want to marry a person who wasn't a realist about life.

"I'm honored you considered me," she said in a neutral tone. What else was there to say to the man who thought it was fine to propose over the phone?

"You consistently made my shortlist when I looked at all of the factors," he said with what sounded like a hint of pride. "Do you have any objections?"

Pearla was sitting at her desk in her large corner office. The room was dark blue and grey, and her desk was a large mahogany antique. Her suit was black and loose, obscuring any hint of the woman beneath it. Did she have any objects?

"I need to think about this. It's sudden."

"No, no, no, I understand. You want to talk to your lawyers and make sure this is a good fiscal move. I get that. So what we'll do is we'll have an engagement party. If by the time the party comes, and you're not satisfied, we'll break it off. It will be an excellent social boost for us both. I'm sure your lawyers will be okay with me. If you can get your background check done in three weeks, I'll set up the engagement party.

"Lance, can we talk about this?"

"Of course, we can meet up later. I always knew you were a logical woman. I'm sure this will work for us both. I've picked the caterer for our event. I hear he's the best. I don't know his name offhand, but he's giving a class tonight. I'll have my EA get you into tonight's class. Offer him whatever, price isn't an issue. I'm leaving to seal a big deal in the morning, but when I come back, we can talk."

"Lance maybe we can—"

"I'm sorry. I have to take the other line. I'll call you later."

Three hours later, the address of the class was sent to her. Pearla looked at the address and the time and realized that by the time she got there, the class would be over. Still, someone had gone through the effort of sending the invite, and politeness was too ingrained in her to simply not go. That was her problem all the way around—she never wanted to offend anyone. In business, they all thought she was a master negotiator, but, in truth, she compromised to avoid long conflict.

Pearla knew the nickname others had given her was Ice Queen. It had more to do with her being unshakeable at meetings no matter how loud anyone else got. She used the moniker as a shield. She wasn't rude, and she never raised her voice. She was the child of a French father who thought it was undignified to yell and a Chinese mother who thought it was unbecoming a woman to argue about anything. Even after the business deal of marriage was proposed, she went back to her calendar and finished her tasks for the day.

Project management had never been her dream job—in fact, she had never liked it—but she was very good at it. After the passing of her father from a heart attack after college, she had taken her business degree and built a company that would take care of herself and her family. But she spent more time behind her desk than she did talking about projects with people.

Pearla drove her gray Honda civic with the windows down, letting in the fresh August evening air. The seasons were changing, and it was Pearla's favorite time of the year. For her, it was still light jacket weather and a great time to go for long walks. It was the temptation of autumn that was wafting in the wind.

This would have been an excellent evening for a

walk. Instead, Pearla was going to see a caterer about an engagement she hadn't agreed to. This was her life. But catering brought back memories.

Once upon a time, she had thought she was going to be a baker. Her father had been alive then. He had told her that it made sense she wanted to bake—after all, they were French.

That had been a lifetime ago.

Sighing, she brought herself back to the present. She had a plan. She'd meet with the caterer, tell Lance that it hadn't worked out, then schedule a time to cancel this engagement. What she dreaded was coming up with a reason they shouldn't get married. But unfortunately, Lance was right. It made logical sense for them to marry. Her mother would think it was the most responsible and stable thing to do. So uncharacteristic of her father. There wasn't anyone else in her life, so it wasn't like she could say she had other prospects.

She was essentially married to her job. Building a company that employed project managers to deploy across the world took time, dedication, and left nothing for a social life. She attended charities like they were birthday parties—but not dates. If it weren't a fruit, she wouldn't know what a date was. Most of the time, she didn't notice it, but lately, there had been a perfect storm of signs that she should be thinking of marriage, like her mother's morning call.

"Pearla, good morning." Her mother was always straightforward. "I know a nice man. I met his mother, and she says he's a good catch."

Pearla had attended a charity last week, where another woman had slipped her a phone number and a postcard advertisement as she spoke.

"Hello, Ms. Isaacs. I notice you always come to these events alone. I wanted you to know we are a very discreet agency for business professionals like yourself."

"Excuse me?" Pearla remembered asking in confusion.

The statuesque blonde gave a demure laugh. "Please don't be embarrassed. Our companions are professional. They pick you up at your door and leave you at your door. Try it."

The woman had patted Pearla's hand and moved on.

She wasn't lonely, exactly. She spoke to people all day and traveled extensively for her career. Pearla didn't lack mental stimulation. Most importantly, she provided for her family. Her mother and sisters didn't need her as much now, but she was always available for them.

At night her condominium was her sanctuary. It had two bedrooms and a large kitchen, which she used daily. It was true there were some nights after she had created a particularly difficult dish that she wondered what it would be like to serve two plates instead of one. Pearla could plan projects, buildings, schools and help small countries with their infrastructure, but being in a relationship had always gone wrong every time she'd attempted it.

Still, Pearla considered herself fortunate. A light on her dashboard flashed, and she heard the ding of her GPS letting her know she was a block away from her destination. She looked at the clock—the class would have ended five minutes ago. If she were lucky, she'd be able to catch them cleaning up maybe. She was going over her speech in her head.

"Oh, you're busy and don't have time. No worries, I'll convey your regrets," she practiced. She was looking for parking when she saw a car double-parked with its hazards lights on. There were several containers on the side of the vehicle, and as she got closer, she could see the figure was faced away from her and shaking his head. She took a look at the clock. If she was going to have any chance of finding the teacher of this class, she needed to ignore this person who seemed to need help. But then her conscience prodded her. Whoever it was, they were stranded in Queens on a Thursday night. She would hate to be in that predicament, and if she were, she hoped someone would help her.

"If you look the other way and slowly drive by, you could say you didn't see them," that other evil little voice said. She let out a sigh and looked over her shoulder to make sure she wasn't causing an accident by pulling up behind the car. It was ten o'clock. In Queens, you could technically find people out at all times of the night, but on weekdays most people were indoors by ten. The possibility of another person stopping was slim.

Maybe the person knew about the class and could give her the number to contact the teacher. Getting a no on the phone would be significantly less stressful and more manageable. She pulled up behind the vehicle and then reached into her glove compartment for her mace. Helping was good, but she wasn't foolish.

As she approached the red Rav 4, she could see that the back door had been left open. Inside were several containers. Phew, no bodies, she joked to herself. She walked around the vehicle and saw a man leaning under the hood. The driver's side door was open, and she could clearly see a man as he stomped back into the driver's seat and turned the engine. Hearing the churning of an engine that sounded just like the little engine that could, made it clear what was wrong with the car.

She had jumper cables in her car, so there went the possibility that she wouldn't be able to help. It also meant the chances of her meeting the caterer had gone from slim, to none. The good news was it was just a jump. She turned back to her car and then pulled it up next to the Rav 4. She got out of her vehicle and opened her trunk, where her cables lay in a beautiful bag.

At least she hoped they were there. She had seen the floral nylon bag at the store and was immediately drawn to it. The zipper of the bag was a flower petal and the straps that closed over the top of the zipper and fastened to the handle. When she had purchased them the attendant had opened the bag and apologized for the red and black handles on the cable but assured her the color disconnect was necessary. Pearla had bought them just in case, but this would be the first time they would be used. She closed her trunk and called out to the man who was once again under his hood.

"Hello, do you need a jump?" she called out. She stopped a body length away. She wanted to help, but there was still some common sense left in her.

"Do you have cables in that cute box?" he responded. "I left mine to make room for my cases, and now my cases need the cables more than ever."

Pearla was frozen in place. That voice. It was warm like a chocolate lava cake and smooth like the melted middle. All of her concerns about stranger danger went away. Should spray him with mace and leave him the box? She couldn't grab on to a clear course of action. The only thing that kept reverberating through her mind was, she knew that voice.

Then like a bad dream, the pieces started to fall into place. The cases outside of the car. They were food cases. Her coming to a cooking class and Lance wanting the best to cater their event. The voice that she'd never forget.

That voice belonged to Evan Carson. The four-star Michelin chef.

He was also the love of her life.

The one she had walked away from.